Wayman's Ford, the easiest crossing of the Brazos River for the cattle herds trailing north to the Kansas railheads, is controlled by the Pickering brothers. When they try to exert too high a toll for the use of the ford, trouble comes from the Broken U outfit. Killing leads to killing and Dan McCoy, Sheriff of Red Springs, moves in to prevent a full-scale war between the two outfits, but arson, rustling and kidnapping sweeps the Brazos country around Red Springs, before Dan, aided by his deputy Clint Schofield, and the Collins family, finally brings the criminals to justice.

WAYMAN'S FORD

WAYMAN'S FORD

by

Jim Bowden

Dales Large Print Books
Long Preston, North Yorkshire,
BD23 4ND, England.

British Library Cataloguing in Publication Data.

Bowden, Jim
    Wayman's Ford.

    A catalogue record of this book is
    available from the British Library

    ISBN   978-1-84262-644-3 pbk

First published in Great Britain in 1960 by Robert Hale Limited

Copyright © Jim Bowden 1960

Cover illustration © Gordon Crabb by arrangement with
Alison Eldred

The moral right of the author has been asserted

Published in Large Print 2009 by arrangement with
Mr W. D. Spence

Dales Large Print is an imprint of Library Magna Books Ltd.

Printed and bound in Great Britain by
T.J. (International) Ltd., Cornwall, PL28 8RW

Chapter 1

Dan McCoy tall, lean, sheriff of Red Springs, lounged lazily in a chair in front of his office. The town was quiet under the sun which blazed down from a clear sky on to the Texas countryside.

The faint clop of slow ridden horses reached his ears and, surprised that someone should be riding in this heat, he turned his head to see who approached Red Springs by the north road.

His clear steel-blue eyes sharpened as their gaze fastened on three riders who appeared at the end of Main Street. They rode so slowly that their horses' hoofs scarcely puffed the thick dust.

'They're about all in,' whispered Dan half to himself when he saw the men drooping in the saddles.

'Who's all in?' asked Clint Schofield, the leather-faced deputy who lounged half asleep beside Dan and who had been startled when Dan's whisper broke the quietness.

'These three,' replied McCoy indicating

the horsemen.

The older man pushed himself upright in his chair and stared at the three men who were moving slowly along the road.

'Joe Williams, Slim Parker and Clance Martin.' The words escaped from the deputy's lips as if he didn't believe them.

'You're right,' muttered Dan springing to his feet.

'They look as if they've been hit hard,' said Clint climbing out of his chair.

The sheriff's eyes narrowed as he watched the three dust covered, travel-weary men who hung limp in the saddles and hardly bothered to guide their horses.

'These men should be riding in happy, ready to paint the town red after pushing that herd to the Kansas railheads,' said Dan wiping the perspiration from his clear-cut, weather-beaten face.

'It just ain't natural,' muttered the old man stroking his stubbled chin. 'There's something wrong, that's fer certain.'

The two lawmen walked across the boards to meet the three riders who halted their mounts in front of the sheriff.

'Hi, Joe, Slim, Clance,' greeted the sheriff nodding to each of the cowboys. 'You look all in. Where's Wayman?'

Joe returned Dan's greeting with a nod. 'He's dead,' he whispered hoarsely through parched lips.

'Dead!' Dan could hardly believe his ears. He stared incredulously at the three men who slipped wearily from the saddles.

Dan stepped from the sidewalk into the dust of the road.

He grasped Joe's arms. 'Where? How? Who?' The words rapped from his lips.

Joe stared wearily at McCoy and before he could speak Dan apologised. 'Sorry, Joe, you all look as if you've had a tough ride. Come on over to the Silver Dollar for a drink, tell me about it then.'

The three men smiled wearily. 'Thanks, Sheriff,' they murmured and turned to walk across the road. They dragged their feet up the steps on to the sidewalk and pushed open the batwings of the saloon thankful to escape from the burning sun.

There were about twenty men in the Silver Dollar and when the batwings squeaked heads turned to see who had pushed them.

'Slim!'

'Clance!'

'Joe! Have a good trip?'

Greetings were shouted across the room as the three men accompanied by McCoy

9

and Schofield crossed to the polished counter, but the friendly calls and smiles faded when the only reply was a grim nod.

Cowboys looked at each other sensing that something was wrong. Dan ordered five beers, and as he felt the tension in the quietness of the saloon he turned his back to the counter and faced the room.

'Joe tells me that John Wayman is dead,' Dan announced quietly.

A terrible silence greeted these words and it hung for a brief moment across the saloon. Suddenly everyone was talking at once.

Dan held up his hands. 'Quiet, everyone, quiet,' he called, and as the murmuring gradually ceased he continued. 'That's all Joe has told me. As soon as he feels up to it he'll tell me the full story.'

All eyes turned on Joe Williams who had drained his first beer quickly and was now enjoying a second glass. He took a long drink, wiped the back of his hand across his mouth and turned to Dan as cowboys gathered round.

'The drive north went well,' said Joe. 'We reached Kansas in good time and Mister Wayman got a good price for his cattle. He paid off the hired hands and told us we'd have three days in town before we hit the trail back here.' Joe paused, took another drink and looked thoughtfully at the glass as if trying to find the words to describe Wayman's death. 'We were going to meet the boss in the Golden Dice saloon and celebrate the good trip. He got there before us and when we arrived he was dead.' The effort to describe what happened dried Joe's mouth and he called for another drink.

'What had happened?' asked Dan.

'It appears that a couple of cowpokers got into an argument and poor old John Wayman stopped one of the bullets,' replied Williams.

'Who were these two hombres?' queried Dan grimly.

Joe shrugged his shoulders. 'Dunno,' he said. 'Never saw them; they'd disappeared when we got to the saloon. Couple of locals, I figure.'

'Didn't the law do anything?' asked Clint.

'What could the law do?' replied Clance as he rolled a cigarette. 'It was an accident.'

The word of John Wayman's death spread like a prairie fire through Red Springs. The whole town was shocked and mourned the death of this likeable rancher. He had been a tall, broad-shouldered, upright man who had fought in the early days of the West and had come to the rich Brazo grasslands of Texas to find peace and build up a big cattle ranch. He had suffered at the hands of rustlers, fire and drought, but he had always pulled through, a man determined to succeed and in maintaining the way was through hard work had never given himself time to court seriously and marry. Known as a man of fair dealing he was well liked and well known throughout the countryside around Red Springs. He was friend of all and enemy of none and now he was dead – the whole town counted the loss as a personal one.

Dan laid his hand on Joe's shoulder. 'Guess there's no need to tell you how we all feel,' he said. 'You'll be going out to the Bar X and look after things until everything's settled.'

Joe nodded and Dan, accompanied by Clint, left the Silver Dollar.

'This is a bad day for Red Springs,' grunted the old man as they crossed the street.

'Look after things, Clint,' said Dan when they reached the office. 'I'm goin' to see Bob Walker an' then maybe ride out to the Bar X.'

Dan's feet echoed on the wood of the sidewalk as he hurried to Bob Walker's office. The middle-aged, grey-haired lawyer, who was busy at his desk, looked up as Dan opened the door. 'Hello, Dan,' he greeted. 'Come on in.'

'Howdy, Mr Walker,' replied Dan as he seated himself in the chair indicated by the lawyer. He removed his Stetson and wiped his forehead. 'Heard about John Wayman?'

The lawyer nodded. 'Yes,' he replied, 'a bad business, a pity he took that herd himself.'

'He'll be missed around here,' said Dan. 'By the way, did he leave a will with you?'

Walker shook his head. 'No, I was always at him to make one but he'd always put me off saying he wasn't going to die for a long time. As a matter of fact I was coming round to see if you'd ride out to the Bar X and bring back any documents or letters you can find. He may have left a will out there.'

'Right,' said Dan. 'I'll do that.' He pushed himself out of the chair and left the lawyer's office. He hurried back down the street, unhitched his horse from the rail and rode home.

'Hello, darling,' greeted his pretty dark-haired wife Barbara, but her smile disappeared when she saw her husband's serious

13

face. 'Anything wrong?' she asked.

Dan slumped wearily in a chair beside the table. 'John Wayman's dead, killed up in Kansas,' he told her quietly.

The news drew a gasp of horror from Barbara. She sank on to a chair beside Dan. 'What happened?' she asked.

Dan told her the story. 'I'm going out to the ranch,' he concluded. 'John didn't leave a will and Bob Walker wants any documents that are out there. Care to help?'

'Of course I will,' replied Barbara, 'but have some coffee before we go.'

Refreshed by the drink, Dan hitched a horse to the buggy and soon the sheriff and his wife were leaving Red Springs at a brisk trot.

They followed the south road for about a mile before turning off to head towards the Brazo River. The trail took them through lush grasslands and Dan recalled how John Wayman loved to ride through this part of his ranch. The trail ran close to a low bluff and turned at the end of the hill to drop steadily towards Wayman's ranch. As they rounded the bluff Dan pulled his horse to a standstill and gazed across the country before him.

Rolling acres of grassland fell gradually

towards the Brazo River twisting its snake-like way through the Texas countryside. Close to the river Dan could see the long low wooden ranch-house which had been Wayman's home. His eyes narrowed; he half expected to see grey smoke curling from the chimney and the powerful rancher stride from the house. His gaze moved along the river.

'Wal, Babs, John's name will always be on the map,' said Dan nodding towards the ford a short distance from the ranch-house. 'The best crossing of the Brazo for a hundred miles or more and it's already known as Wayman's Ford.'

Barbara nodded. 'A pity he hadn't a son to carry on,' she said sadly.

'Sure is,' replied Dan as he flicked the reins and sent the horse forward at a brisk trot.

'Has he any relatives?' asked Barbara.

'I've heard him speak of a brother back east somewhere but he's never been out here,' answered Dan. 'I hope I can find some information amongst his papers.'

Two hours later Dan and his wife returned to town and the sheriff spent the rest of the day in the company of the town's lawyer going through masses of documents and letters which Dan had found at the ranch.

'Wal,' said Dan as he laid down the last letter, 'there's no will there.'

'Reckon not,' agreed Bob Walker. 'Then I guess I'd better write to John's brother, explain everything and see what he wants to do with the Bar X. Will everything be all right out there?'

'Sure,' said Dan. 'Joe Williams is looking after things.'

'Good, then all we can do is wait,' said Bob.

Almost a fortnight passed before Bob Walker hurried to Dan's office with the news that he had received a letter from John Wayman's brother.

'Wal, when do we see the new owner?' asked Dan eagerly.

'We don't!' announced Walker.

Dan and Clint stared incredulously at each other.

'The man's out of his head with a place like the Bar X to come to,' spluttered Clint.

A smile creased the lined face of the lawyer. 'Don't be too hasty, Clint,' he said. 'Don't forget this man's back east an' it appears from his letter he has no desire to come west.'

'What's goin' to happen, then?' asked the

weather-beaten deputy.

'He wants me to see that the ranch is sold,' replied Walker. 'He's left everything to me but has made one stipulation that the ranch is not sold privately but is auctioned.'

'Umph!' grunted Clint disgustedly. 'Money grabber. He wants it auctioned so's he can get a higher price.'

'A wise precaution,' grinned Bob. 'I could have sold it at a knock-down price to a friend for a nice backhander, couldn't I?'

Clint rubbed his chin and looked at the lawyer wryly.

'Guess you could, but you wouldn't,' he said.

'No, I wouldn't,' agreed Walker, 'but John's brother doesn't know me.'

'You'll fix everything up,' said Dan. 'When do you reckon on having the sale?'

'As soon as possible,' answered the lawyer. 'Let's say a week next Friday; that'll give us plenty of time to get notices out.'

The day of the sale brought more activity to Red Springs than it had seen for many a day. The town, recovered from the shock of John Wayman's death, now looked upon the sale of his ranch as a gala day. People from miles around were using it as an excuse to come to town for it was known that several ranchers were interested in the property and the sale promised some excitement. Wives encouraged their menfolk to come as it meant they would get an extra visit to town and see if the stores had 'the latest from back east.' The men needed little persuasion for they saw a chance to drink with old friends. Red Springs set itself out to cater for the influx and the chance to get extra cash into town made the townsfolk build the occasion into something of a gala. Bets were even being made as to who would get the Bar X, but the favourite was Bill Collins, the sheriff's father-in-law, who had a ranch close to town. It was known that he had been looking round for another place and the Bar X would suit him admirably.

Dan and Clint strolled casually along the sidewalk eyeing the sudden increase in Red Springs population with wary eyes.

'Jest as well you swore in a few more deputies for the day,' grunted Clint.

Dan smiled. 'I figured this might happen,' he said. 'Reckon we'll have a few drunks,' he added as they passed the Silver Dollar.

'As long as they don't all git the idea they can shoot,' snorted Clint, 'I don't mind.'

The two lawmen reached the office and flopped into the chairs on the sidewalk.

'Reckon we can watch the comings and goings from here for the next two hours,' said Dan pushing his Stetson to the back of his head.

Dan reckoned he had been sitting there about an hour when his attention was drawn to two men riding slowly into town. They were strangers to him and their dust-covered horses showed every sign of a long ride. The two men were in marked contrast. The short, stocky but powerfully built man was dark and his upper lip was covered by a thick black moustache. The other rider was tall and thin and his fair hair which crowned a thin, drawn face was in need of cutting. The dust of a long trail covered them so that the colour of their well-worn clothes was hardly distinguishable.

They looked around them as they rode slowly along Main Street and Dan reckoned they were wondering why so many people moved in a town the size of Red Springs.

The riders pulled up in front of the saloon, climbed slowly out of the saddles and after hitching their horses on to the rail strolled into the Silver Dollar which was packed with cowboys. They walked slowly to the bar and ordered two beers.

'What goes on?' asked the dark man when

the bartender returned with the drinks.

The barman looked at the two cowboys in amazement but did not speak.

The dark man repeated his question quietly and added, 'Why so many folks in town?'

'Haven't you heard or seen any notices?' asked the bartender.

'I wouldn't have asked you if we knew,' snapped the moustached man.

'The Bar X is up for sale today,' replied the barman, who pulled a notice from under the counter and then hurried to serve someone further down the bar.

The two men read the notice before speaking.

'Guess we got here jest in time,' muttered the thin-faced cowboy. 'There's sure goin' to be a surprise for little old Red Springs.' He grinned at his companion.

'Careful what you say,' snapped the other man. 'You talk too much at times. C'm on, finish your drink an' let's go find a sheriff or lawyer or somethin'!'

They drained their glasses and left the saloon. The batwings were still swinging behind them when they stopped a cowboy on the sidewalk.

'Where can I find the sheriff or a lawyer?'

asked the dark man.

'Over there,' answered the cowboy indicating the sheriff sitting outside his office across the street. 'That's him, an' that's Bob Walker, our local lawyer, talkin' to him.'

'Thanks,' came the reply and the two men stepped down into the dust of the street.

As Dan was talking to Bob Walker he looked up and was surprised to see the two strangers walking across the street obviously heading in his direction. He straightened in his chair and eyed them curiously.

'Howdy, Sheriff,' greeted the short, stocky man. 'I'd like a word with you. And your friend,' he added as Bob Walker made to move away. 'I've jest had you pointed out as the town's lawyer and my business concerns you as well.'

Walker showed some surprise and glanced at Dan.

'Way off your own beat, aren't you?' drawled Dan noting the accent of a Kansan.

'Guess we are,' returned the newcomer, 'but this'll be our beat in future so we'd better introduce ourselves. I'm Matt Pickering an' this is my brother Luke.'

Dan nodded. 'Glad to know you,' he said. 'This is Bob Walker, and Clint Schofield.' The four men accepted each other's greeting without any ceremony and Clint watched the Pickering brothers carefully, studying them shrewdly through narrowed eyes.

'Your last remark seems to mean you going to be staying around here awhile,' observed Dan.

The brothers grinned at each other. 'That's shore an understatement,' guffawed Luke. 'We're goin' to be around permanent.'

'Yeah, an' there seems to be a lot of folks around here getting excited over nothing,' laughed Matt.

'What do you mean?' asked Dan suspiciously.

'Wal, that property we've seen billed is not for sale,' announced Matt.'

'Not for sale?' said the astonished Bob Walker. 'Of course it is, the late–'

'Now that's where you're wrong,' interrupted Luke leaning forward, one foot on the sidewalk. 'Show him, Matt,' he added, turning to his brother who pulled a piece of paper from his pocket and handed it to Dan without a word.

Silently the sheriff unfolded it. He stared at the paper hardly able to believe what he saw. He looked up at the Kansans and handed it to Walker without speaking.

The lawyer gasped. 'This is a bill of sale

for the Bar X!'

'Yeah. That's right,' grinned Luke.

Clint Schofield jumped from his chair. 'What!' he gasped. 'Wayman would never sell the Bar X.'

'Is that Wayman's signature, Bob?' asked Dan calmly.

'I'd swear it was,' answered the lawyer examining the signature carefully. 'But I'd like to check it with some I have in the office.' He looked questioningly at the two brothers.

'Shore that's all right,' replied Matt. 'Examine what you like; you'll find everythin' in order.'

The five men walked along the sidewalk to the lawyer's office, Clint bringing up the rear muttering under his breath that the whole thing was impossible. As the office door shut behind them Luke turned to Clint.

'Look here, old man,' he snapped jabbing a finger in Clint's chest, 'I don't like the way you're muttering about this being impossible. Get this straight, the Bar X belongs to us and we have documents to prove it.'

Clint looked shrewdly at the thin-faced Kansan. 'I guess you have, but Wayman's riders knew nothin' of this sale and, by the way, what happened to the money you paid for it?'

Dan glanced sharply at his deputy realising that Clint was suspicious. Before Dan could speak Matt Pickering answered Clint. 'How should we know what Wayman did with his money; let's find him and ask him.'

The three men stared at the two brothers incredulously and then glanced sharply at each other.

'What's the matter?' snapped Luke.

'Didn't you know Wayman was killed up in Kansas?' asked Dan quietly.

'What!' gasped Matt with surprise. 'But we arranged to be here today to take over. We've heard nothing about a killing. What happened?'

After Dan had related the story of Wayman's death Matt Pickering looked thoughtful.

'If Wayman's riders knew nothing of the sale then this must have happened very soon after we made the deal, before he'd had time to meet them.' A frown creased Pickering's forehead as he stared at the ground. 'It's the cash that puzzles me.'

'That was an awful lot of money to hand over in ready cash,' commented Clint.

'Yeah, I reckon it was,' agreed Matt. 'Wayman insisted on cash. I tried to talk him out of it but he wouldn't hear of it. It so happened we had enough cash from a big sale of cattle we'd just made and we hadn't got it to the bank.'

'Then where was it when John was killed?'

'Your guess is as good as mine,' said Matt.

'Maybe whoever examined the body saw it and made of his chance,' suggested Luke.

'I guess that isn't impossible,' answered Dan.

'Wal,' said Matt casually, 'I guess that's no concern of ours. I figure we'll find our way around the ranch.'

Dan turned to Bob Walker who had been examining several documents. 'Well, Bob?'

The lawyer looked up from the papers. 'Everything seems to be in order, this is John's signature all right.'

'We told you that,' sneered Luke.

'Wal, I guess I'll hev my papers back and head for the ranch,' grinned Matt Pickering, as he plucked the documents from the lawyer's hand with a gesture of finality.

The brothers strode to the door. Matt paused, his hand on the knob. He turned still grinning. 'Better stop that sale, Sheriff,' he said.

Chapter 2

The three men stared as the door slammed behind the Pickering brothers.

'Wal, I'll be darned,' murmured Clint.

Bob Walker shook his head. 'I'd never have believed John Wayman would sell the Bar X.'

Clint Schofield stroked his stubbled chin thoughtfully. 'You know, I've a feeling I've seen those two before.'

Dan looked sharply at his deputy. 'Where?' he asked.

Clint shook his head. 'That's just it, I jest can't place them, but there's something familiar about that fair-haired hombre.'

A puzzled furrow creased Dan's forehead. 'Can't say I've seen 'em,' he observed, 'but it may be worth keeping tag on them. Bob, will you stop the sale? Clint, we'll rid to the Bar X. I haven't seen Joe Williams and the boys in town yet so there might be trouble out there when those Kansans ride in.'

Dan left for the office, followed by Clint, and their feet echoed on the wood as they hurried along the sidewalk to their horses. As the lawmen swung into the saddle, they noticed the Pickering brothers were leaving the Main Street by the south road, and turning their horses they followed the two men.

The Pickerings kept a steady pace, and the lawmen had no difficulty in keeping them in sight. Clint was the first to break the silence when they were half way to the ranch.

'These two brothers seem to be familiar with this ride,' he said.

'Jest what I was thinking,' replied Dan, 'but of course they could have had instructions how to get to the ranch.'

Clint grunted and tried to remember where he had seen the brothers before.

As soon as the ranch was in sight, and the ground dropped away to the Brazo, the Pickerings put their horses into a fast gallop and were soon riding up the avenue of cottonwoods to the ranch-house.

The sound of the hoofs pounding the hard ground brought out Joe Williams and the other Bar X men. They stared curiously at the two riders who pulled their horses to a sliding halt in front of them. Matt and Luke swung from the saddles and tossed the reins to one of the cowboys.

'Bed 'em down,' ordered Matt.

The cowboy stiffened and let the reins drop.

Matt stopped in the act of turning to Joe Williams who stood a little in front of the other men. He looked sharply at the cowboy. 'I said bed 'em down,' he rapped with a menacing voice.

Joe Williams stepped forward. 'These boys take orders only from me,' he said coolly.

'That so,' smiled Luke mockingly.

Joe's eyes narrowed. 'Yeah,' he drawled quietly. 'No stranger comes here throwing his weight around, least of all a Kansan.'

Matt stepped close to Joe. 'You'd better tell that cowboy to do as his boss tells him,' he hissed.

'He does what I tell him,' answered Joe.

Luke started to laugh and Joe stepped past Matt. 'What's so funny about that?' he snapped.

'Jest that you aren't the boss,' replied Luke. 'We are!'

Joe gasped, glancing sharply from one brother to the other. 'Quit jokin',' he hissed. 'The sale hasn't started yet.'

'There isn't going to be a sale,' replied Luke.

'No sale?' frowned Joe. 'What are you

gettin' at?'

'Jest that Wayman sold the Bar X to us up in Kansas,' said Matt smoothly.

'What!' Joe gasped incredulously and a murmur of astonishment ran through the group of cowboys. 'He didn't tell us and I–'

He never got a chance,' interrupted Matt, 'from what I hear he was killed jest after he sold us his spread.'

Joe's eyes narrowed; he looked suspiciously at the brothers. 'You can prove it, I expect?' he queried.

'Sure we can and have already done so to the sheriff and lawyer in Red Springs,' replied Matt, a note of triumph in his voice.

Williams looked shrewdly at the two men. 'Could hev been a frame up by a couple of murderin' Kansans,' he muttered viciously.

Anger flowed in Matt's dark eyes. He stepped forward swiftly and smashed his fist into Joe's face sending him crashing to the ground. Dazed by the blow, the foreman shook his head and wiped the blood from his mouth with the back of his hand. He glared at Pickering, hate smouldering in his eyes.

The Bar X cowboys started to move towards the two men but found themselves looking into the cold muzzle of the Colt which had leaped into Luke's hand.

'All right, easy off,' ordered Luke coldly.

Matt plucked his sombrero from his head and threw it to one side. 'I see I'm goin' to have to teach you Texans some manners,' he said menacingly.

Joe pushed himself to his feet, swaying from side to side, but before he could straighten Pickering lashed him with another vicious blow to the head which spun him backwards. He crashed into the water trough, lost his balance and tumbled over the side, sending water flying in all directions. Joe gasped for breath as the coldness hit his body and penetrated his humming brain. The sudden shock helped to revive him and he saw clearly the grinning face of the dark Kansan. He pulled himself to his feet and hurled himself from the trough taking Matt by surprise. Joe's full fifteen stones smashed into the Kansan and both men crashed to the hard ground. Joe seized his advantage and pounded his fist into Matt's face. The Kansan yelled with pain but rolled to one side before Joe could get a firm grip on him. Quick as lightning he was on his feet and kicked viciously at the Texan who had half lunged to his feet. Joe saw the kick coming and halted his step. His broad hands grasped Matt by the ankle and with a quick jerk threw the Kansan to the ground. He leaped forward only to be met by Matt's upraised knee. The blow caught Joe in the pit of the stomach, halting him in his tracks with a yell of pain. Matt scrambled to his feet as Joe sank to the ground and he was about to leap forward when the crash of a Colt split the air.

Pickering spun on his heels to see Dan McCoy and Clint Schofield galloping towards them, guns raised. They brought their horses to a halt in front of the group of men.

'All right,' snapped Dan. 'Break it up.' He turned to Luke. 'An' you'd better put that gun away.'

Luke grinned at the sheriff and slipped his Colt back into its holster.

'We soon meet again, Sheriff,' panted Matt Pickering leaning on the water trough and wiping his hand across his face.

'Seems my hunch was right that there'd be trouble when you got out here,' said Dan. 'Take Joe inside,' he ordered, turning to the Bar X riders who were already helping their foreman to his feet.

Joe, his face twisted with pain, looked at Dan. 'Is it right,' he gasped, 'that these coyotes own the Bar X?'

'Seems like it,' nodded Dan.

Joe's face clouded with disgust: he said nothing but as he turned he spat viciously into the dust.

'Hold it,' rapped Mat Pickering turning to face the cowboys. 'You haven't heard everything. Tomorrow my own outfit from Kansas will be here so I want all you men off the place in the morning.'

The men gasped, looking at each other in amazement.

'We'll be off in an hour,' snapped Joe. 'We've been in your company too long.'

The Bar X hands turned away and walked dejectedly to the bunk-house.

Dan was about to speak but Luke interposed. 'Save your breath, Sheriff, there isn't anything you can do about it. There's no law to say who a man hires.'

'No, there isn't,' agreed Dan calmly. He leaned forward in his saddle. 'But let me warn you,' he continued icily, 'I'll not stand fer trouble from you or your outfit. You seem way out of place down here. I can't turn you off because you're Kansans, but step out of line an' I'll–' Dan left the implication of his words to the men's imagination and, pulling his horse round, sent it forward to leave the Bar X.

'Aren't we goin' to stick around until the boys leave?' asked Clint anxiously as he drew alongside the sheriff.

'There'll be no more trouble out here today,' replied Dan turning on to the trail to Red Springs.

Two hours later Dan was in his office studying the latest 'wanted' posters. The town was quiet but suddenly the stillness was broken by intermittent shouting which came from away down the sidewalk. Gradually it became more insistent until it began to sweep along the street like a wave. Dan hurried to the window. 'What's goin' on?' he muttered to himself when he saw a large group of cowboys splitting up and hurrying to their horses. He gasped when he saw Joe Williams and the Bar X riders being swept along by the crowd. Soon horses were milling around outside the saloon sending the dust swirling in clouds from the main street. Suddenly the door burst open and Clint rushed in gasping for breath.

'Trouble, Dan,' he panted. 'Thet mob's aimin' to run the Pickerings out of town.'

Dan rushed outside. Already the riders, yelling to each other, were turning their horses. The sheriff ran into the middle of the road waving his arms and yelling at the top of his voice. The ground shook as the riders put their mounts into a full gallop. Dan realised he was too late but he drew his Colt in one last effort to stop the mad rush. The Colt roared above the noise of the hoofs and several horses faltered momentarily only to be driven onward by the swirl of the animals behind them. Dan saw the ride was not to be stopped and flung himself sideways as the horses thundered down on him. He hit the dust and crashed into a sidewalk as the riders pounded past.

He picked himself up slowly. 'Fools,' he spat. Retrieving his Stetson, he turned to see Clint unhitching the horses from the rail.

'You all right?' asked Clint.

Dan nodded, grasping the reins which Clint handed to him. They leaped into the saddle and, kicking their horses into a fast gallop, rode through the dust swirling along the south road out of Red Springs. Dan flattened himself on his horse calling it to greater effort. He knew that with men in such an ugly mood, the Pickerings could suffer worse than being run off the Bar X.

After about two miles, Dan realised he had gained little on the riders ahead and that if he kept the same trail he would not catch them before they reached the ranch. He pulled hard on the reins bringing the horse sliding in the dust. As Clint drew alongside Dan yelled, 'We'll have to cut over the bluff.'

Almost before the horses had stopped the two men pulled them round, pushed them forward into a fast gallop away from the trail to head for the hills. Soon they were climbing steadily and as the ground became steeper their progress became slower. They twisted and turned up the hillside and as they climbed higher the path narrowed. Dan kept glancing anxiously at the dust cloud which marked the progress of the men from Red Springs following the trail which swung round the far end of the hill which Dan and Clint were climbing. The urge to hurry their horses onwards was great, but both men realised that they must conserve energy for the ride once they had reached the top. Suddenly, the path narrowed and ran forward about a hundred yards as a ledge along a cliff-like face. The lawmen slipped from the saddle and led their horses forward, calming and encouraging them with soothing words.

Clint's horse proved to be more nervous and in one moment when its back feet sent stones clattering over the edge of the ledge, the deputy thought the animal was going to panic. Clint's soothing voice caressed the animal and gradually it calmed down enough for him to lead it forward. Once across the ledge the path turned steeply to the top of the hill where the two men swung quickly into the saddles and kicked their horses into a fast gallop across the hills which after two miles dropped gently to the Brazo River. Dan did not spare the horses now but kept them at an earth-shaking pace, sending dust flying as they hurtled across the ground. They thundered on to the trail and Dan felt some measure of relief when he saw the dust cloud still rising beyond the bluff.

'We've made it,' he yelled to Clint, driving his horse along the trail to the ranch.

The sound of the hard-ridden horses brought the Pickering brothers hurrying from the ranch-house. The lawmen pulled their mounts to a dust-swirling halt in front of the veranda and were out of the saddles almost before the animals had stopped.

'What brings you here again in a mighty hurry?' asked the surprised Matt.

'That,' answering Dan pointing at the gang of riders who were now in sight on the trail from Red Springs.

'What's on?' snapped Luke.

Clint eyed him shrewdly. 'Jest these folk

aim to run you out of here but the sheriff thought it his duty to protect you.'

'Protect us,' sneered Luke pulling his Colt from his holster and examining the chamber. 'We don't need wet nursing.'

Dan stepped forward and snatched the gun from Luke's hand. 'Protect you, yes,' he rapped. 'I saw the mood of the mob before they left Red Springs. Things could get out of hand, but there'll be no shooting for either of you.' he turned quickly to Matt and relieved him of his Colt.

Luke's eyes narrowed. 'I get it now, you disarm us on the pretext of protecting us, and then you'll let those dirty Texan friends of yours take us,' he snarled accusingly.

Clint jumped forward and smashed his fist into Luke's face, sending him reeling into the dust. The deputy stood over him, his feet astride. 'Sheriff McCoy's as straight as a die,' he hissed. 'He'll do what he think's right and that don't include approving of mobs.' Clint looked hard at Luke who climbed slowly to his feet. 'I didn't like the look of you when I saw you ride into Red Springs. I like the look of you even less now, but you're on the right side of the law as far as we know so we'll jest do our duty as we see it.'

Dan made no comment, but turned to

Matt. 'You two get inside and keep out of sight and keep that brother of yours quiet.'

Hot words sprang to Luke's lips but his brother stopped him and indicated the door. The two lawmen watched them go inside before stepping on to the veranda and turning to see the horsemen who thundered towards the ranch-house.

'Where's the two Kansan coyotes?' shouted the leading rider as they pulled up in a swirling cloud of dust. 'Out of the way, Sheriff, and let's have them.' The men from Red Springs yelled their approval.

'You aren't taking anybody,' answered Dan shaking his head.

'We don't want any thieving Kansans around here,' someone yelled.

'They aren't thieves,' shouted Dan.

'How did they get the Bar X?'

'Probably murdered John Wayman as well.'

Everyone seemed to be yelling at once. Dan drew his Colt, raised it skywards and squeezed the trigger. The roar of the gun jolted everyone and the shouts died away.

'The Pickerings have documents to prove that John Wayman sold them the Bar X,' the sheriff shouted. 'I've seen them, so has Clint and Bob Walker. Everything is in order so you can forget the whole thing and get back to town.'

Some hothead at the back of the mob did not heed Dan's words. 'Look what they did to Joe Williams,' he yelled.

An angry murmur ran through the men. 'Let's get 'em,' someone shouted. The men moved forward menacingly. A gun appeared, but before the trigger could be squeezed Dan's Colt crashed, sending the weapon spinning from the rider's hand. The mob halted as one man.

'Anyone wanting the Pickerings will have to pass us first,' Dan called.

'Protecting stinking Kansans,' yelled the leader. The shout against the sheriff was taken up on all sides.

'I'm protectin' you as well,' shouted Dan. 'I'm stoppin' you from making a big mistake. If you'd got these men an' anything had happened to them you'd have all been responsible!'

The shouts began to die down as the implication of Dan's words began to make themselves felt in their angry minds.

'These men have done nothing wrong,' continued Dan. 'They're here legal like an' you may as well accept the fact that they're likely to be here for some time. They own

the Bar X and are goin' to be our neighbours. As Sheriff, I uphold the law, be it
Texan or Kansan thet's in the wrong. Now
turn those horses an' ride back to town an'
cool off.'

For a moment no one moved: angry
glances were thrown at the lawmen and
strong murmurs of disapproval ran through
the mob, but slowly the Red Springs men
pulled their horses round and trotted away
from the ranch.

As the riders disappeared the ranch-house
door was flung open and the Pickering
brothers reappeared.

'Thanks, Sheriff,' muttered Matt. 'Thet
could hev been an ugly situation if you
hadn't been here.'

'You should have let us teach them a
lesson,' snapped Luke.

'Small chance you'd hev had with that lot,'
answered Clint.

'I'd advise you to keep away from Red
Springs for a while,' said Dan. 'At least until
tempers settle down. Better warn your outfit
when they get here. Let the townsfolk get
used to you being around.'

'Sure, Sheriff, we'll do that,' answered
Matt accepting his Colt from Dan. 'We only
want things to run peaceable.'

The lawmen climbed on to their horses and with a brief nod to the two men rode slowly through the line of cottonwoods and turned on to the trail to Red Springs.

'Think they suspect anythin'?' asked Luke as he watched them go.

'How can they?' replied Matt firmly. 'Those documents fooled them. If we play things steady then we're in for some big money. C'm on, let's have a look at the ford.'

The two men walked to the Brazo River and viewed the crossing with interested eyes.

'We'll get the boys started as soon as they're settled in,' said Matt, 'and then we'll be ready for the herds moving through here in a couple of months' time.'

Luke laughed. 'Some drovers are in for a shock.'

The next day Red Springs turned out to see the arrival of the Kansans and Dan was prepared for trouble but he noted with satisfaction that Matt Pickering rode with his outfit.

'Must hev by-passed town to meet them,' commented Dan.

Here and there an odd word of abuse was flung at the newcomers, but generally their arrival was greeted with silence.

'All credit to Pickering,' said Dan as the last of the outfit left Main Street and headed along the south road. 'He's kept a tight hold on his men an' they were raring to reply to those taunts.'

Clint grunted in reply. 'I've a nose for trouble, an' I smell it comin',' he warned.

'No reason why it should,' answered Dan turning to his office.

A week later when Dan and Clint were riding along the banks of the Brazo they decided to call at the Bar X before returning to town.

'I think it's time we paid the Pickerings a visit to see how they are getting on,' said Dan. 'We've had no trouble from them yet,' he added with a grin at his deputy.

They rode steadily along the river bank but when they came in sight of the ford Dan reined his horse to a halt with a gasp of surprise. On either side of the river fences had been erected forming a funnel down to the ford.

'What's goin' on?' asked Clint.

'Seems you were right, Clint,' answered Dan grimly. 'There's all the makings of big trouble there. By using those funnels the herds crossin' Wayman's Ford can be counted: that means Pickering wants to know the numbers and that can only mean one thing – a toll.'

Clint gasped. 'Then we're in fer a rough time. The drovers aren't goin' to like this.'

'C'm on,' said Dan. 'We'll pay Matt Pickering a call.'

The lawmen kicked their horses forward and were soon greeting Matt Pickering in front of the house.

'Howdy, Sheriff,' welcomed Matt. 'Are your neighbours peaceful enough?'

Dan leaned forward in the saddle. 'I haven't any complaints and folks in town seem to have settled down.'

'Then the boys can come into town?' asked Matt.

'Sure,' replied Dan, 'but warn 'em to tread lightly.'

Pickering nodded.

'You've been making a few changes around here,' continued Dan nodding in the direction of the ford.

'Yeah,' grinned Matt. 'Reckoned that the ford could bring in a tidy sum of money if we charged for the use of it.'

Dan frowned. 'That smells like trouble to me,' he said grimly. 'Nobody's goin' to like it.'

'They'll hev to pay and like it,' replied

Matt, 'or go further south.'

'The next ford's over a hundred miles away, across poor grazing country, an' you know it,' snapped Dan.

'Then they'll have to pay up,' replied Matt smoothly.

'The trail drovers are goin' to be sore: Wayman allowed free use of the ford,' said Clint.

'Wayman isn't running this ranch any more,' snarled Pickering, 'an' I'm charging. It's legal so you take care of any trouble-makers.' He swung on his heels and strode into the house.

Dan pulled his horse round in disgust and the two lawmen rode back to Red Springs.

As the weeks moved by Dan kept check on the herds moving towards the Brazo and, anticipating trouble when they reached Way-man's Ford, he swore in as special deputies Bill Collins and his two sons Jack and How-ard. To their surprise the expected trouble did not materialise. There were protesta-tions, grumblings, and harsh words, but in the majority of cases the trail drivers paid up. Some turned back to take their herds a hundred miles along the Brazo, but word came through that they had been jumped by Pancho Gonzales, a Mexican rustler, who had moved into Texas. Dan spent weeks in the hills trying to trace Gonzales but without success, and other ranchers paid the toll rather than risk losing their cattle.

'Seems as though the Pickerings have won out on this idea,' mused Dan.

'Reckon so this year, ' replied Clint, 'but I wouldn't bet on next year – the Broken U hasn't been through this time an' thet's some big tough outfit with Brooks at their head. When he and Pickering meet there could be one big explosion.'

Chapter 3

'Hold it!' The stern voice rasped across the Silver Dollar saloon.

Mick Wilson's hand froze on the butt of his colt slung low on his right thigh. He turned his head to see Dan McCoy, a tall, lithe cowboy, standing beside a table a few yards away. A sheriff's badge gleamed on his brown shirt. Steel-blue eyes gleamed steadily from a clean-cut, weather-beaten face, watching every movement of the two men who had run foul of each other.

'Draw, an' I'll blast daylight into you, Mick,' warned the sheriff, his hand poised close to his holster.

Wilson's eyes narrowed; his face lost its colour; his lips trembled. Even though he was already touching his Colt he knew that the sheriff, Dan McCoy, would beat him to the draw. Anger darkened his eyes.

'Might hev known you Texans would hang together,' he snarled as his hand slipped from his gun.

The sheriff relaxed and walked across to Wilson.

'It's not a question of hangin' together, Mick, an' you know it. I'll hev no gunplay in this town if I can prevent it.' He turned to the other cowboy who faced Wilson. 'An' thet goes fer you too. 'Fraid I don't know your name.'

'Jed Burrows, Sheriff,' drawled the short, thick-set cowboy, eyeing Dan carefully. He saw a man of about twenty-five, good-looking in a rugged way. He noted the guns hanging low on his hips held firm by a thin leather thong round the legs. Here was a man who was used to drawing his guns; a gunfighter on the right side of the law. 'Trail herdin' fer the Broken U outfit,' he added.

'Thet the herd thet's jest crossed Wayman's Ford?'

'Yea,' Wilson broke in. 'An' thet's the cause of the trouble. I don't mind him protestin' but when he starts gettin' personal about my bosses an' worse still about Kansas, well–'

'If it's so good why don't you go back there?' rasped Jed. 'We'd be better off without you an' those two thievin' bosses of yours.'

Wilson's lips tightened; his eyes narrowed.

'That'll do,' snapped McCoy. 'Any more of this an' I'll clap you both in jail until you cool off.'

'All right, Sheriff,' drawled Jed, 'but you must agree thet a dollar a head for cattle to use Wayman's Ford is robbery an' I figure thet thieves should git what's comin' to 'em.'

'Shore, shore, thieves should,' agreed Sheriff McCoy, 'but then the Pickering brothers ain't thieves.'

'Now don't tell me that you agree with those low down rattlesnakes. Ask any rancher, trail boss or trail herder thet's used Wayman's Ford what they think to the brothers an'–'

'I know, I've heard all this a year ago when the Pickerings moved in,' cut in Dan. 'But the whole thing depends which way you

47

look at it. You say it's too much an' they probably think it's too cheap.'

'An what do you say, Sheriff?'

'I ain't here to take sides, Burrows. I'm here to see thet there's peace an' everythin' is run legal like.'

'Legal like,' Jed Burrows sneered. 'Thet's all you lawmen think about – not what's fair. But I warn you we ain't the only outfit thet don't like it. There's trouble comin'.' He tossed back his whisky and without a further word stormed out of the Silver Dollar.

Dan McCoy watched him go and as he swung back to the bar Mick Wilson turned to leave. Dan stopped him.

'I think you'd better stay here with me fer a while. We'll let thet trailer git out of here an' out of gunshot.'

Wilson quirked his eyebrows. 'You can't make me stay, Sheriff.'

'Try me an' see,' drawled Dan quietly.

The cowboy turned back to the bar. 'Give me another whisky,' he called angrily.

Dan smiled to himself although his thoughts were troubled. This little tiff was nothing compared to what could happen unless something could be done about the levy on the use of the ford.

McCoy's thoughts were interrupted. 'C'n I go now, Sheriff?' muttered the man at his side.

'Shore, I guess Burrows will hev quit town.'

Wilson turned without another word and strode from the saloon. The batwings were still swinging when the blasting roar of a Colt shook the occupants of the Silver Dollar. They jumped to the windows but McCoy was the first to the batwings. He crashed through them, his .45 leaping to his hand.

Few people moved on the street but the lifeless form of Mick Wilson lay in the dust of the road beside his horse tied to the hitching rail. His gun was still in its holster. He hadn't had a chance. Dan rose slowly from his knee after giving the body a quick glance. He turned, his eyes probing for the killer. Suddenly he froze. Slowly he mounted the steps back on to the sidewalk. His footsteps echoed on the wood as he moved grim-faced towards Jed Burrows standing a few yards along the boards. Dan did not speak but with a swift movement jerked the cowpoke's gun from its holster. He glanced at the muzzle and held it to his nose but it was neither warm nor smelt of powder. He twisted the chamber and six bullets rattled on the sidewalk.

He glanced at Burrows and the grin which met him brought a coldness to his eyes which forbode ill for the murderer. He looked hard and long at the trail herder, then shoved the Colt back into its holster.

'Thanks, Sheriff,' mocked Burrows. 'Find what you want?'

'You know I didn't. But by the body that lies there I will. I reckon you know more about this than you'd care to tell, Burrows.'

He glanced at the Texan, then swung off the sidewalk and hurried across the street to his office. Clint Schofield, Dan's deputy, stood outside. The shot had brought him hurrying from the desk, but when he saw that Dan was already in the street he had kept a watchful eye in case of further trouble. The sheriff entered the office and after a cursory glance up and down the street Clint followed him.

'Wal, Clint, it's happened.'

Clint nodded as he chewed at his tobacco. 'Guess we always knew it would.'

'Suppose it hed to sooner or later when the Pickerings put a ford toll on. I'm surprised it didn't happen last year.'

'Don't see what we can do about it,' observed the grizzled-faced deputy. 'It's all legal like.'

'Shore, but we'll hev to do something or there'll be a war on our hands. Reckon I'll mosey over to the Pickerings an' hev a word with 'em.' Dan picked up his brown Stetson. His face was grim as he added, 'First I'll call on the Broken U outfit.'

'Want me along, Dan?' queried Clint eagerly.

'Shore, c'm on,' smiled Dan. 'I know you'd rather be in the saddle smellin' out trouble than sittin' behind thet thar desk.'

Clint grinned, passed a rifle to Dan and followed him outside. The street was quiet once again and there was no sign that a few minutes ago blood had stained the dust.

The two lawmen unhitched their horses, swung into the saddles and left Red Springs by the south road at a steady lope.

Not a word was spoken as they rode along. Each was lost with his own grim thoughts. The leather-faced deputy glanced at his young companion. He saw a clean-cut, weather-beaten face full of determination; steel-blue eyes missing nothing on the trail. Two years had passed since Dan had returned to Red Springs and cleaned up the Griffiths-Brown gang to reinstate himself as a sheriff. Those two years had been peaceful but for some time Clint had seen trouble brewing over Wayman's Ford.

The two men turned off the south road and cut across the grassland.

'Guess thet'll be the Broken U,' shouted Dan nodding in the direction of a cloud of dust rising in the distance.

'Reckon so,' answered Clint. 'It's the only outfit in these parts. The Crooked A is still two days' ride from the ford.'

Dan pushed his horse forward. The black, clean-limbed animal stretched its legs but Dan checked its urge to break into a gallop. The sheriff knew his mount and held to a steady pace, conserving its strength in case extra effort should be needed later. The two riders pulled to a halt at the top of a slight rise. Below them in a shallow bowl of grassland the Broken U outfit was encamped. The large herd of steers was quiet and under the perfect control of the trail herders. Dan stiffened as he looked at the camp. The cowboys were standing around a rider astride a big powerful horse. Dan sensed something was amiss; he had a feeling that orders were being issued which spelt trouble.

'C'm on,' he yelled to Clint and kicked his horse into a gallop. Clint wheeled his horse round and stabbed it forward after the black which stretched itself across the ground in a dust-raising gallop.

Dan watched the encampment carefully. They had covered about a quarter of the distance to the camp when he saw the cowboys run to their horses. He drew a sharp breath of annoyance and called on his horse for greater speed. Clint followed Dan's example, flattened himself in the saddle and pushed his horse alongside Dan as they raced towards the Broken U outfit. Dan narrowed his eyes. He saw the cowpunchers climb into the leather and wheel their mounts after the man who had already been in the saddle and who was now leaving the camp at a steady but urgent gallop towards the Brazo River.

Dan nodded to his deputy and as one they turned their horses across country. Grass and earth flew as hoofs pounded the ground in urgent gallop. The ground rose steadily away from the hollow for about a mile but the pace did not slacken. The two riders did not falter as they topped the rise but urged their horses faster over the grassland which sloped gently to the Brazo River five miles away. Dan saw they had gained on the Broken U riders and turned his horse to cut them off before they reached Pickering's spread.

Suddenly Clint yelled and pointed across the sloping country. Dan started. A posse of horsemen were riding away from the river! Dan cursed loudly and with a yell flattened himself along the horse's back and stabbed it forward to greater speed. The earth shook beneath the pounding hoofs.

'Take the Broken U, Clint,' shouted Dan. 'I'll take the Pickerings.'

Clint's call was lost on the wind as Dan changed the direction of his gallop. He concentrated on his ride; all thoughts driven from his mind but the one urgent need to stop these two parties of riders meeting. The black answered his call and the powerful animal lengthened its stride seeming to hardly touch the ground as its supple legs drove it forward.

Clouds of dust swirled maliciously behind the two groups of horsemen as they approached each other with thoughts of death in their minds. Dan could almost sense their feelings as he carefully weighed up the distances. He saw that Clint was rapidly approaching the Broken U outfit but his face was grim as he saw the Pickering riders quicken their pace. Quickly he swung his horse to allow for this change. The distance closed rapidly. He noticed that Clint had reached the trail and had turned to face the oncoming Broken U riders.

Clint breathed a sigh of relief as he pulled his horse to a sliding dust-raising halt on the trail. He turned quickly and held the panting, snorting animal steady to face the thundering riders who approached rapidly. Pulling his Colt from its holster he saw the pace of the Broken U falter. Their leader held up his hand and the bunch slowly came to stop in front of Clint whose star shone brightly on his chest to give him the authority to question the hard-headed bunch of Texans.

'What the hell do you want, tin star?' asked the leader, his face black with annoyance at the interruption.

'Jest you sit tight there awhile. You ain't meetin' the Pickering outfit without the sheriff. There's goin' to be no bloodshed here if we can help it.'

'Thet's just what there is goin' to be if those Kansans keep chargin' ford toll.'

Clint did not answer as he watched the tall, broad powerfully-built leader. Years of experience had taught Clint to weigh men up quickly and now he saw a man who was tough and used to having his own way; a man who went along with the law but who was not afraid to take matters into his own hands if he thought the law inadequate. Well dressed in every-day working clothes, he was obviously a man of influence in his own part of Texas. Clint smiled grimly to himself.

'Wal,' drawled the tall rider, 'you goin' to let us pass, lawman?'

'Nope,' answered Clint quietly, 'leastways not until the sheriff says so, an' I'm shore goin' to see thet he gits his chance to say his piece.' He nodded in the direction of the hard-riding horseman who hit the trail in a thundering gallop about a quarter of a mile away.

As he slid in front of the Pickering outfit Dan yelled to them to halt, a gun leaping to his hand. The star and the Colt had their effect and the Pickering brothers called their riders to a halt.

'Hold it!' shouted Dan. 'You ain't meetin' the Broken U with guns blazin'.'

Matt Pickering, short, dark moustached elder brother, leaned forward, hand resting on his saddle. He looked straight at Dan, his voice quiet but full of meaning. 'Blaze they will at those murderin' coyotes.'

Dan eased himself in the saddle. 'News shore travels fast in these parts but the killer of Mick Wilson won't go unarrested.'

The tall, thin-faced Luke Pickering studied the sheriff carefully.

'Then you know who did it?' he asked.

'No.' Dan shook his head. 'But I aim to find out,' he added grimly.

Luke laughed. 'Thought not,' he mocked as he spat in the dust. 'You lawmen are all alike. Out of our path an' we'll take care of this in our own way.'

Dan stiffened. 'Stay where you are. I'm handlin' this killin'.' He motioned menacingly with his gun.

Luke glanced at Matt who still leaned forward in his saddle. He shook his head. 'Better do as he says, Luke.' He turned to Dan. 'If you don't git results then you can expect us ridin' after the Broken U outfit. All right, men, you can go back now.'

Dan breathed a sigh of relief. His hard ride had not been in vain. As the cowboys turned their horses he called to Matt.

'I want you an' your brother to ride with me to the Broken U along there.'

'All right,' agreed Matt, 'but I don't see what good thet's goin' to do you.'

'Jest come along without your comments,' answered Dan slipping his Colt back into its holster.

The three men rode slowly along the trail

and pulled to a halt alongside Clint.

'Good work, Clint,' said Dan. 'Reckon we didn't ride fer nothin'.' He watched the bunch of horsemen carefully before turning his attention to their leader.

'Guess you must be Al Brooks, boss of the Broken U.'

'Yeah, you shore is smart, Sheriff,' mocked the rancher. 'Guess thet took a lot of figurin' out.'

Dan's eyes narrowed. 'See here, Brooks, you may be a big shot down where you come from but around here I'm the law an' whilst you're passin' through my territory you're jest another cowpoke to me.'

The rancher stiffened. 'Them's bold words, kid, an'–'

The words were lost as Clint's Colt snapped forth and a gun spun into the dust, blasted from a cowpoke's hand. Like a flash of lightning Dan's .45 had leaped into his hand.

'Keep your hands off those guns!' he snapped. Every hand in the party froze to the butts jutting from their holsters. 'The next one might git a bullet somewhere else.' Dan's voice went quiet as he turned to Brooks. 'I'm warnin' you, see thet your men behave themselves, we've had one killin' by your outfit already an' I don't figure on havin' any more.'

'Any proof?' asked the rancher, a glint in his eye which made Dan eager to smash his fist into the Texan's face.

'No,' Dan answered controlling himself. 'But when I hev I'm comin' after the man thet did it. Now send your cowpokes back to camp but you an' your foreman stay here.'

After a moment's thought Brooks dismissed his men then swung on Dan.

'What you goin' to do about this ford toll?' he snapped.

'Thet's legal,' cut in Matt Pickering before Dan could reply. 'Ain't thet so, Sheriff?'

'Shore is,' agreed Dan.

'Sidin' with Kansans!' stormed Brooks. 'You ought to be horsewhipped.'

'Thet don't enter into it,' replied Dan. 'I don't agree with what the Pickerings hev done but there isn't anythin' I can do about it.'

'Wal if you can't we herders will,' threatened Brooks.

'Shore,' smiled Luke Pickering, 'you can go a hundred miles further south to cross the Brazo.'

Brooks's face darkened. 'You know thet'd

cost us more than crossin' Wayman's Ford an' thet the grazin's not so good.'

'Then pay your toll like a good boy,' laughed Matt. 'An' I figure every time the Broken U comes through here in future they'll pay fifty cents a head extra to go to poor Mick Wilson's widow, eh, Luke?'

'Shore,' nodded the thin-faced cowboy with a grin.

'Why, you low-down, good-fer-nothin'–' spluttered Brooks, his hand moving towards his holster.

'Leave it,' snapped Dan. 'You'll pay when you cross here an' like it until things alter.'

'I'll see them Pickerings dead before I'll pay another cent. Red,' he turned to his foreman, 'send one of the boys back down the trail an' warn the oncomin' herds to try the south road an' tell 'em why. I'll see you make no more out of this ford, Pickering!' He hurled his horse round in fury and kicked it into a gallop, followed by his foreman. The animals leaped forward and Dan's face was grim as he watched the dust whirl upwards behind the galloping figures.

A smile broke across Matt Pickering's sun-browned face. 'They'll soon tire of thet southern trail, eh, Luke?'

'Shore will,' grinned Luke turning his

horse. 'So long, Sheriff.'

'Hold it, Luke, you too, Matt,' called Dan. 'Can't you drop this ford charge? Oh, I know it's legal,' he went on seeing the protests rising to the lips of the brothers, 'but it's hard on the southern ranchers an' it appears is going to lead to trouble. Why don't you be content with ranchin'; the Bar X is one of the best spreads around here?'

Before he received an answer Clint spoke, 'John Wayman had no need of it, he let the ranchers use the ford for nothin' an' everythin'–'

'More fool him, he would hev made a packet,' snapped Luke.

'Pity he got killed. This trouble wouldn't hev arisen if he'd been here.'

'Reckon not,' answered Mat. 'But then he isn't an' we are, an' we are goin' to run this as we like.'

'Yeah, providin' you keep on the right side of the law, Pickerin',' drawled Dan. 'Jest see thet you do.'

A smile flicked across Matt's face as he pulled his horse round. 'Sheriff, see thet you git a man fer Mick Wilson's murder or we'll be ridin' agin an' git one fer ourselves.' He shoved his horse forward.

'So long again, Sheriff,' drawled Luke tipping his Stetson in mock salute. 'Be seein' you.'

'C'm on, Clint, we'll go straight to the hornets' nest fer this here murderer,' he said, wheeling his horse in the direction of the Broken U encampment.

Chapter 4

'We shore won't be welcome at the Broken U,' commented Clint pulling his horse alongside Dan's.

'Reckon not,' mused Dan, 'but thet's the best place to start. Jed Burrows knows more about this than appears. Whilst I'm quizzin' him you take the trail to Red Springs an' see if you can pick up any signs on the number of riders thet went to town this mornin'.'

The older man nodded. 'Wonder why they picked on Mick Wilson?' he grunted, stroking his stubbled chin.

'Thet's what puzzles me. Could hev been jest to draw Pickerings into fightin' or maybe somethin' happened at the ford thet we don't know about.'

'The Pickerings are slippery customers if I

62

knows my men,' muttered Clint.

Dan nodded and eased his well-worn sombrero on his head. 'There's one thing I can't figure about those two, Clint, it's worried me for the past year.' Dan's brow puckered as he paused and Clint glanced at the young Sheriff.

'Wal?' he asked.

'They're Kansans an' it's a mighty long way to come to settle down here, especially if it's right thet they hed a thrivin' ranch up north. Apart from which they arrived here at the right time – jest after news came back of John Wayman's death, an' the ranch was up fer sale.'

Clint stiffened in his saddle. 'Thet's something thet's always puzzled me. Coincidence?' The old cowboy scratched his lined forehead. 'I've always thought thet I've seen those two before but I reckon my memory ain't what it used to be.'

The lawmen fell silent, relaxing in the saddles and letting their horses ease their way along the trail after the hard gallop.

The low moan of cattle drifted on the breeze as the two riders neared the camp which was still hidden from view by the rise ahead. Dan checked the hang of his Colts and eased himself in his saddle. Suddenly he pulled his black to a stop.

'Here's someone in a hurry,' observed Clint reining his grey alongside Dan.

A cowboy, crouching in the saddle, had galloped over the rise from the direction of the camp. Unhesitatingly he pounded down the trail quirting his horse to greater speed. The lawmen watched without a word. Hoofs thrumming the ground whirled dust behind him. Without altering his pace he thundered towards the watching men who held their horses steady, waiting for any reaction from the rider to their presence. But it was as if they had not existed. With no more than a glance at the lawmen the cowboy thundered past. Dan and Clint turned in their saddles and watched the rider disappear in a cloud of dust which rose behind him.

'That hombre means to git there fast,' said Clint.

'Guess that's the rider Brooks ordered back to the herds trailin' up behind him.'

'Yeah an' he means to use Wayman's Ford.'

Dan nodded and kicked his horse forward. Soon they were dropping into the Broken U camp and cowboys gathered round as they stopped in front of Brooks.

The rancher grinned broadly. 'Wal if it

ain't the kid lawman looked after by pa.'

Dan ignored the remark. He glanced round the cowhands laughing at their boss's greeting.

'You, Jed Burrows,' snapped Dan, 'c'm here. I want a word with you.'

Grins disappeared as Dan's voice lashed over their heads. He noticed Burrows glance quickly at Brooks.

'You've no right comin' here demandin' like this,' protested Brooks sharply. 'I won't—'

'Brooks,' cut in Dan leaning forward in his saddle, 'I'll hev no more of you tellin' me what to do. I've every right as a law officer investigatin' a murder so you can send these other cowpokes packin' whilst I talk to Burrows.'

All the cowboys turned to look at their boss. The situation was charged with tension; a nod from Brooks and lead would fly. The sheriff moved his hand to the butt of his Colt; beside him he heard the ominous click as Clint cocked his rifle. Brooks heard it too. Suddenly he swung round and chastised his men.

'C'm on, what you standing around fer? You heard the sheriff. You've all got plenty to do. Git back to your work.' He paused, waving his arms at his men. Slowly they turned heel and shuffled away. 'Not you, Burrows,' snapped Brooks. 'Sheriff wants a word with you.'

'Thanks, Brooks,' said Dan swinging from the saddle. 'Thet was mighty sensible of you. Jest carry on as if we weren't here.'

He turned to Burrows and took him to one side. For a moment he did not speak.

Suddenly he snapped. 'Who killed Mick Wilson?'

Jed Burrows grinned as he hitched up his trousers. 'Tryin' to take me unawares, Sheriff? Won't work 'cause I don't know.'

'I figure different,' answered Dan. 'Anyone ride into town with you this morning?'

'Did you see anyone, Sheriff?' countered Jed quietly, his voice indicating a man who was sure of his ground. Dan knew he would get nothing from the man who casually rolled himself a cigarette, but he figured that Burrows knew whose bullet had killed Mick Wilson.

'All right, Burrows, thet'll do fer now,' said Dan.

'Thet was short,' answered the cowboy. 'An' sweet,' he added, his eyes mocking the young sheriff. He sauntered away whilst Dan hurried to Brooks.

'Anyone leave this camp this morning?' he asked.

'Shore,' drawled the rancher. 'I sent Burrows into town to do a job fer me.'

'What sort of job?' queried Dan.

'Thet's my private business,' countered the rancher.

'Wouldn't be to kill a man, would it?'

'Got proof it was?' mocked Brooks knowing full well that Dan had nothing to substantiate his theory.

'Anyone ride with Burrows?'

'No, no need, besides I wanted the rest of the hands here.'

Dan muttered his thanks and turned to Clint who was still seated on his horse. Holding on to a stirrup he whispered to his deputy who leaned from the saddle to catch his words.

'Examine thet trail. I'll nose around here and wait fer you. Be back in an hour.'

As Dan stepped back Clint pulled his horse round and rode out of camp along the trail to Red Springs.

Dan spent the next hour nosing for information. He thought a casual question here and there might bring an unguarded answer, but the Broken U outfit were not to be caught and if they were to be believed only Jed Burrows left camp that morning. The hour passed and Dan grew somewhat anxious. Clint was not one to be late. A further fifteen minutes passed and Dan was worried. He had ceased his investigation and anxiously watched the trail along which he knew Clint must return.

'Still hangin' around, lawman,' grinned Brooks, thumbs holed in his belt as he sauntered up to the sheriff. 'What you expect to happen now?'

'Jest waitin' fer my deputy to show up,' answered Dan quietly, not betraying the anxiety which filled his mind. 'Reckon he'll use thet trail so I may as well ride to meet him.'

'Shore, call again sometime, kid,' Brooks said as Dan swung into the saddle.

The sheriff turned his horse without a word and rode out of camp. Once out of sight Dan urged his horse forward, quickly covering the ground. Two miles from the camp he steadied his mount where the trail wound through some low hillocks which broke the flatness eight miles from Red Springs. Rounding a bend in the trail Dan gasped and kicked his horse into an urgent gallop.

He hauled sharply on the reins when he

reached a figure prostrate in the dust of the trail. Dan leaped from the saddle before the black had time to stop. He flung the reins loose and the animal trotted slowly in the direction of a horse which champed the grass beside the trail. Dan dropped on to his knees beside the still form. Firmly but gently he turned the man on to his back.

'Clint!' gasped Dan.

He stared at the deep furrow oozing blood across the white forehead. Lifting him in his powerful arms Dan carried the unconscious deputy to the shadow of the hill. He laid him down gently and ran to his horse. Pulling out his canteen of water Dan hurried back to the wounded man. Easing Clint's head upwards he forced some water between the parched lips. He unfastened the neckerchief, soaked it with water and after carefully wiping the wound tied the cloth round Clint's head.

The task completed the sheriff set off to collect the horses. He had gone only a few steps when a low moan made him spin on his heels. Clint stirred; his eyes flickered open. Dan sprang to his side.

'Clint! Clint! How do you feel?' he called eagerly.

The older man stared at him with unrecognising eyes. Nausea gripped Dan's stomach at the thought of his old friend with a lost memory.

'Clint, it's me, Dan.' He gripped Clint by the arms.

The wounded man gazed at the young sheriff for a moment. Slowly recognition crept into his eyes. Dan relaxed his grip; a long sigh escaped his lips.

The sheriff pressed the canteen to Clint's mouth, and the older man drank eagerly.

'Dan,' Clint whispered. 'Glad to see you.' Slowly he lifted his hand to his forehead. 'How bad is it, Dan?'

'You're lucky to be here. A fraction of an inch further an' you'd be dead. I reckon a couple of days will see you on your feet again.'

Relieved at the news Clint sank back against the ground.

'Who did it?' Dan asked grimly.

'Dunno,' answered Clint. 'I was examining the trail as I rode back, spotted somethin' hereabouts an' hed jest got on to my knees when I glimpsed a rifle pokin' over yon hillock.' Clint paused to take another drink. He wiped the back of his hand across his lips and continued. 'I moved sideways but reckon I wasn't quick enough. The shot must hev knocked me out an' maybe saved my life –

expect the coyote thought he'd got me an' didn't bother further.'

'You didn't see anybody?'

'No.'

'Guess someone must hev followed you from the camp. What did you find on the trail?'

'There were two sets of fresh tracks headin' fer town an' one was made by a horse with a broken shoe on his front left leg.'

Dan gasped. 'Good man, Clint. Now we've got somethin' to work on. Think you can ride into town with my help?'

'Shore, but thet's wastin' time, Dan. Leave me here an' git back to the Broken U an' look fer a horse with a broken shoe before they alter it.'

Dan nodded. 'You be all right?'

'Shore, pick me up on the way back.' Clint looked at Dan as he hesitated. 'Go on, git off with you, don't waste time.'

Dan smiled. 'Be back soon.' He ran to his horse, leaped into the saddle, waved a greeting to Clint and kicked his horse into a gallop along the trail to the Broken U camp.

'Now what?' snapped Brooks with annoyance as Dan slipped from the saddle.

'Jest hev your men show me their saddle horses,' ordered Dan.

Brooks stared at the sheriff. 'You've no right–' He stopped when he saw the muzzle of a Colt pointing at his stomach.

'Move,' hissed Dan. 'I haven't time to waste.'

Brooks glared at the young sheriff, then called to his men to bring their horses forward. One by one Dan examined their front legs. When the last horse had been taken away he turned to the Broken U boss.

'Thanks,' he said casually, slipping his Colt back into its holster. 'You've been mighty obligin'.'

He moved forward only to be stopped as Brooks grabbed his arm.

'What's the idea?' snapped the rancher.

'Jest curious,' grinned Dan.

'Find what you wanted?'

'We'll see.'

Dan's smile and evasive answer angered the Texan. He glared at the sheriff. 'Don't come snoopin' round here agin,' he hissed between clenched teeth. 'I won't answer for what might happen.'

Dan did not answer but swung into the saddle, kicked his horse forward and left the camp.

'Find anythin'?' asked Clint eagerly as Dan jumped from his horse.

'No broken shoe,' Dan replied, smiling at the disappointment in Clint's eyes. 'But,' he continued, 'I found a horse with a new shoe on his left front leg.'

Clint jumped up excitedly. 'That'll be him! Let's go git him. Why don't you pull him in?'

'Not so fast, old timer,' cautioned Dan. 'It's no proof thet he was Mick Wilson's killer.'

Dan laughed when Clint screwed up his face with disgust. 'Arrest 'em first an' then ask your questions.'

'Couldn't hold him, Clint, an' you know it, but I made a note of what thet hombre looks like.'

'C'm on then,' shouted Clint. 'Let's hightail it to town an' check with old Silas Garnett if he's shod any horses this morning.' The deputy sheriff hauled himself on to his horse and in spite of a throbbing head pushed his horse into a gallop towards Red Springs.

Dan grinned at the enthusiasm of the old timer and spurred his horse alongside Clint.

They covered the ground quickly and soon hauled their sweating horses to a halt outside Silas Garnett's blacksmith's shop. They leaped from their saddles and hurried

73

inside to find Silas shoeing a horse. He glanced up when he heard the quick step of the two lawmen.

'Howdy, Sheriff,' he greeted. 'Clint, old timer, what you been runnin' into?'

Clint spat on the ground. 'Some murderin' coyote.'

Silas glanced sharply at Dan. 'Know who it was?'

'No, but we think you can help us.'

'Me? Wal, I ain't been out of this shop, all day.'

'Thet's just it, Silas. You see we figure thet the hombre we want also killed Mick Wilson an' we reckon he's one of the Broken U outfit. The only thing we hev to go on is a broken horseshoe – left front leg. There's a horse in Broken U camp with a new shoe on that leg. Did you shoe a horse this mornin', Silas?'

'Yeah, four,' answered the blacksmith. He rubbed his chin thoughtfully. 'Let me see now, one was fer Doc an'–' A low whistle escaped from his lips; his eyes lit up excitedly. 'I've got it. Two fellahs, never seen 'em before, came in here, one of their horses had a broken shoe, wanted it doin' right away. I obliged. They seemed a bit on edge, kept tellin' me to hurry an' one of 'em kept a watch along the street as if lookin' fer someone. As they were leavin' they asked if I knew if Mick Wilson was in town.' He paused for breath.

'What were they like, Silas?' asked Dan eagerly.

'Wal, one was–'

His voice was halted by the roar of a Colt. The shot crashed round the shop. Silas grasped at his chest, coughed, slipped to the ground and lay still.

Chapter 5

Dan spun on his heels and ran to the door drawing his Colt. Cowboys ran towards the blacksmith's shop but there was no sign of the killer. Clint was beside him muttering vengeance on the murderer.

'Take thet way, Clint,' ordered Dan.

Clint hurried cautiously down the street whilst Dan worked carefully along in the opposite direction. A few minutes later both were back outside the blacksmith's shop where already cowboys were taking the dead Silas away.

'Find anything?' asked Dan anxiously.

The older man shook his head, a disappointed look covered his face. 'No,' he replied. 'Did you?'

'Not a sign. Guess the killer disappeared into some buildin'. He could easily give us the slip in some of these alleyways.'

'What now, Dan?' asked Clint.

'I reckon this confirms our suspicious of the Broken U, but the evidence we need is jest as far away as ever. We'll jest hev to play a waitin' an' watchin' game.' Dan's serious tone brightened a little as he turned on Clint. 'But first we've got to hev you seen to. A visit to the Doc's an' then a rest.'

'I'm all right,' protested Clint.

'Wal, you don't seem to hev weathered too badly considerin' all the excitement we've had,' grinned Dan, 'but all the same we'll take precautions. C'm on.'

Dan led the protesting deputy to see the doctor who reported that Clint would soon be all right if he took things easy for a couple of days.

Having made Clint promise to carry out the doctor's orders, Dan hurried home where he found his pretty wife, Barbara, anxiously awaiting his return.

'Heard there'd been a bit of trouble an'

that you had ridden out of town. Dan, I was worried.'

Dan smiled as he took his wife in his arms. 'It's my job, Babs, an' I'm afraid there's goin' to be trouble.'

Barbara raised her head from the safe, comforting feeling of Dan's broad chest. She gazed up into the steel-blue eyes as Dan fondled her hair. Her brow furrowed with a troubled frown.

'Oh, no!' she whispered.

Dan brushed away the frown with his long supple fingers.

'Thet frown is unbecomin' to such a pretty face,' he said. 'Don't worry,' he continued, 'everything will be all right.'

'Can't help it, Dan. I don't want to be left a widow. I thought we'd finished with trouble when you stamped out Griffiths and Brown. What is it now?'

The sheriff quickly related the happenings.

'I've been expectin' this ever since the Pickerings moved in. Pity your Dad didn't get a chance to buy the Bar X when we heard about poor old John Wayman.'

Barbara nodded. 'He would have done if there'd been a sale, but the Pickerings beat him to it.' She looked thoughtful. 'You know, Dan, it has often struck me as strange that those two should arrive here all the way from Kansas and produce a bill of sale on the day of the auction.'

Dan glanced sharply at his wife. 'You, too. I've often wondered an' Clint voiced the same thoughts this mornin'.'

Their conversation was interrupted by the sound of a hard-ridden horse. As one they moved quickly to the window.

'It's Jack,' whispered Barbara recognising her brother.

'Wonder what's wrong,' puzzled Dan striding towards the door.

He flung it open and hurried to meet the rider who pulled to a sliding halt, jumped from the saddle and leaped the low fence.

'Look as if the devil was chasin' you,' called the sheriff as Jack Collins ran towards him.

'Jest seen a cold-blooded shootin', Dan,' panted Jack.

Dan was startled. 'Another?' he gasped. 'Where was this?'

'Yon side of Wayman's Ford. Lone rider was bushwacked by four of Pickering's cowpokes.' Jack looked puzzled as he looked at Dan. 'What do you mean, another?'

'There's been two killin's already and

Clint's been wounded.'

It was Jack's turn to be startled. 'What's goin' on?' he asked as they entered the house. 'All was peaceful like when I left town early this morning.'

'Tell you about it in a minute, Jack. Give me your story first,' replied Dan.

Jack nodded his thanks as he gratefully accepted the steaming coffee which his sister offered him.

'Wal, I went south of the Brazo to look over some land thet Dad's thinkin' of buyin'. I was on my way back, nearin' Sundance Hollow. I saw this fella comin' hell for leather an' reined in to watch him. Seemed as if he was on somethin' mighty important. Wal, jest as he reached the bottom of the Hollow these four hombres jumped him. He never hed a chance. I couldn't do a thing; didn't see 'em until they'd got him an' then they were away in a mighty rush.'

'But you recognised them?' asked Dan anxiously.

'Shore, like I told you they were Pickering's cowpokes. No need to disguise yourself when the man you're after isn't goin' to live to testify an' you're bushwackin' him on a lonely trail. It was jest their bad luck thet I happened along.'

'Shore was,' agreed Dan. 'Know the cowboy they killed?'

Jack shook his head as he sipped his coffee. 'No, never seen him before but I can give you a description. I figure he'd be about twenty-five, tall in the saddle, rode thet horse as if he knew how.'

'What was he wearin'?' cut in Dan.

'Dusty brown sombrero, blue jeans an' scarred leather chaps, but the thing which really distinguished him was his red shirt an' of course his black horse which hed a white star on its forehead.'

Dan slapped the table hard. 'Thet's him!' he yelled excitedly.

'You know him, Dan?' asked Barbara.

'Saw him this mornin'. He came from the Broken U outfit an' he passed Clint an' me jest out of their camp,' replied Dan. His face grew grim as he turned to Jack. 'This is a killin' fer revenge. Mick Wilson was shot down this mornin'. I figure it was the Broken U behind it but can't prove it. This herder's used Wayman's Ford, been spotted an' these four coyotes hev cut across to Sundance Hollow to git him in revenge fer Mick Wilson's killin'.'

Jack whistled. 'You're goin' to hev a war on your hands, Dan.' He looked curiously at the sheriff. 'You said there hed been two killin's?'

Dan nodded. 'Yeah, but I'll tell you about all thet as we ride.' Dan fastened on his gun belt and he asked. 'You willin' to testify against these gun-men?'

'Shore, Dan, shore.'

'Then c'm on. I'm goin' to arrest them.' Dan picked up his Stetson and turned to the door. Jack followed him. Barbara rushed to them as Dan opened the door.

'Be careful, both of you,' she said anxiously.

Jack patted her arm as he stepped past Dan. 'Now, sis, don't worry.'

Dan's grim face managed a smile as he bent forward to kiss Barbara lightly. 'Be back soon, sweetheart.' He swung round without a further word and quickly climbed into the saddle.

Tears were in Barbara's eyes as she watched the two cowboys ride away.

On Jack's suggestion they picked up his brother, Howard, before they left town. Grim faced, the three cowboys rode at a steady canter along the south road out of Red Springs. Three miles along the trail they cut across country in the direction of the Brazo River. Swinging round the bluffs they saw the ranch-house and buildings of the Bar X spread lying peacefully under the hot sun and a short distance away the Brazo flowed over the shallows which were the cause of all the trouble – Wayman's Ford.

There was no sign of life as the three riders approached the ranch, but as they swung out of the saddles in front of the veranda a door opened and Matt Pickering stepped out.

'Wal, if it isn't the sheriff. We're seein' a lot of you today,' grinned Matt.

'Yeah,' answered Dan grimly, 'an' you're likely to see a lot more.'

'Good,' laughed the Kansan, 'thet'll be our pleasure. C'm on in.'

'No, thanks,' replied Dan. 'I want to see Shorty Rawlings, Zeke Flint, Walt Stewart an' Buck Taylor.'

Matt Pickering's grin vanished. He looked puzzled when he spoke. 'What's the game, Sheriff, what you want them fer?'

'Jest a case of murder!'

Pickering stared at Dan. 'What you mean? You don't think they killed their own buddy.'

'I wasn't referin' to Mick Wilson. C'm on, Pickering, where are they?'

'They ain't here, Sheriff. I sent 'em out the

other side of the river to check on the oncomin' outfits an' their herds an' to warn 'em about the toll.'

'You expectin' them to use Wayman's Ford, then?' questioned Dan.

'Of course I do,' answered Matt. 'Why shouldn't they?'

'You heard Brooks tell his foreman to send a cowpoke to tell 'em all to go south an' not cross here.'

'Course I did, but you don't expect 'em to go all that way south, do you?' grinned Matt, pulling at his moustache.

'Could do,' replied Dan.

Pickering laughed loudly. 'Guess you don't know thet route, McCoy. They'll come through here all right.'

'Guess you're right.' Dan's voice was quiet. Suddenly it snapped like a whip-lash. ''Cause you know thet the Broken U rider won't git to meet 'em.'

Matt Pickering looked as if a thunderbolt had hit him. Dan watched him carefully, looking for some sign which would indicate how much this Kansan knew. But there was nothing to show whether Pickering was playing a game or was genuinely surprised at the news.

'What you mean?' Matt parried.

'You know what I mean,' snapped Dan. 'The Broken U hombre was bushwacked in Sundance Hollow by your four cowpokes.'

'First I've heard of it,' answered Pickering calmly, his face impassive. 'How do you know it was them?'

'Witness,' pointed out Dan.

Horses' hoofs clopped the ground and the cowboys in front of the veranda swung round to see who was approaching. Slowly Dan turned back to the dark Kansan. He eyed him suspiciously.

'Thought you said these four coyotes were riding to check the herds?'

Pickering mumbled as he glared at Dan. 'Somethin' must hev brought 'em back. Why aren't you checkin' the herds, Shorty?' he called as the dust-stained riders pulled up.

Dan noted the puzzled looks cross the faces of the men still in the saddles. Matt Pickering saw it too and before any of them could speak he continued.

'Thought you wouldn't be back 'till late after lookin' over the outfits an' their steers.'

The man addressed as Shorty lived up to his name and was slovenly dressed in working clothes. Dan watched him carefully, noting the worn butt of the Colt which hung

84

low on his leg. He was quick to follow the lead given by his boss.

'Wal, boss, we expected to find the first outfit nearin' Sundance Hollow, but it wasn't even in sight so we figured we could give it another day.'

Matt Pickering nodded. 'Jest as well,' he said. 'Cookie'll rustle you some grub if you let him know you're back.'

'Right, boss,' replied Shorty pulling his horse round.

'Hold it,' rapped Dan in a commanding voice. 'You been in Sundance Hollow?'

The four riders stopped as one. Dan noted the sharp glances which passed between Pickering and his cowboys.

'Wal, not in it, only near it,' drawled Shorty.

'See anythin' of a lone rider?' asked the sheriff.

'Nope.' Shorty spat on the ground.

'You seem to be doin' all the talkin'. What about you fellas?' He turned his attention to the other three riders who muttered that they had seen no one.

Dan tensed himself anticipating trouble. His arms hung loosely by his sides, his hands close to his holsters. His eyes narrowed.

'You're liars as well as murderers,' he

snapped. The four riders stared at him unable to believe their ears. 'You were seen to bushwack a lone rider,' continued Dan, 'an' he was from the Broken U.'

'Got what he deserved if he was from thet outfit,' snarled Shorty, 'but we didn't do it.'

'You were seen,' replied Dan.

'Who saw us?' asked Shorty. 'These hombres I expect or else they wouldn't be here.'

'Thet's right,' answered Dan quietly. 'Jack Collins was out thet way.'

'Wal, he won't testify,' snarled Shorty. His hand flashed to his gun but Dan was just that shade quicker and before Shorty could press the trigger his wrist was shattered. The gun spun from his grasp into the dust.

'Thet was mighty stupid of you,' snapped Dan. 'Don't anyone else try it,' he warned, but Shorty's companions were already staring into the cold muzzles of the Colts held by the Collins brothers.

Dan watched Matt Pickering carefully but the boss of the Bar X did not move a muscle.

'Wal,' drawled Dan, 'seems I was right about the killin'. We're takin' 'em in fer trial.'

Whilst Jack kept the killers covered Howard removed their guns. The three men from Red Springs swung into their saddles.

'McCoy,' called Pickering, 'you're arrestin' my riders fer a killin' but I ain't heard of you arrestin' any of the Broken U fer killin' Mick Wilson. Seems you might hev favourites.' Pickering's eyes narrowed. 'Be careful, McCoy,' he hissed. 'You haven't heard the last of this.'

The sheriff ignored the boss of the Bar X and motioned his prisoners forward.

Chapter 6

Jed Burrows pushed through the batwings of the Silver Dollar saloon and breathed deeply of the fresh air which met him. Behind him shouts and laughter mingled with the buzz of conversation. In the background an old piano wheezed fitfully. The cowboy hitched up his belt, stepped forward on to the dusty road and untied his horse from the rail.

He was about to climb into the saddle when he noticed a procession of seven horsemen moving slowly along the street. There was a certain grimness about the way they rode and Burrows noticed that the four who were grouped close together rode dejectedly whilst the other three behind and on either side of the first group were upright in the saddle and rode with a purpose in their carriage.

Jed narrowed his eyes as he stood still holding the reins.

'McCoy,' he whispered to himself. 'Who's he pullin' in?'

At that moment the batwings of the Silver Dollar squeaked to eject two cowboys. They paused when they stepped on to the sidewalk. They were about to walk away when they spotted the little cavalcade approaching the sheriff's office.

'McCoy's goin' to fill his jail,' observed one.

'What's been happenin'?' queried the other.

'Old man Collins told me his son hed witnessed a killin' out at Sundance Hollow. Four of Pickering's cowpokes bushwacked some hombre out there an' McCoy figures it was a rider from the Broken U outfit.'

'Guess maybe it was revenge fer the killin' of Mick Wilson.'

'McCoy's goin' to hev to move sharp or there's goin' to be big trouble.'

The two cowboys strolled along the sidewalk but Jed Burrows had heard enough to make him leap into the saddle and leave town at a dust-stirring, trail-pounding gallop.

He quirked his horse calling for greater speed and did not ease his gallop until he reached the camp. His yells brought the trail herders running from their various jobs. He pulled hard on the reins to bring his horse sliding in the dust to stop in front of his boss.

'Mr Brooks,' yelled Burrows jumping from the saddle. 'Al Saunders murdered.'

'What?' shouted Brooks, anger flaring in his face.

A murmur ran round the cowboys before everyone started to shout at once.

'Quiet,' called Brooks. 'Let's hear Jed's story.'

'Four Bar X riders jumped Al south of the Brazo. Some hombre name of Collins saw them so the sheriff has pulled them in.'

Angry shouts broke from the crowd.

'Let's get 'em!'

'Don't take it lyin' down, boss!'

'Burn up the Bar X spread!'

Brooks jumped on to a box. 'All right, quiet now, everyone. First, we aren't goin' to take this lyin' down.' With everyone yelling at this announcement a few moments passed before Brooks could continue. 'Al must hev been spotted when he crossed the ford an' they knew we were sendin' someone to warn the other outfits on the trail so they saw he didn't git through. I'm still bent on gittin' word to those outfits, especially our own second drag thet's next herd but one down the trail, an' so spoil the pleasant Mister Pickering's toll. Duke, take the best horse we hev an' git word through – send 'em south; swim the river further down; don't use the ford.'

Duke nodded his understanding and hurriedly left the crowd.

'The rest of us will ride into Red Springs!'

A cheer broke from the cowboys, but as they turned away Brooks stopped them. 'We'll not go before dark an' Mister Sheriff hed better not be in our way this time!'

Dan McCoy looked worried when he entered his office after putting the prisoners safely behind bars.

'Thanks fer your help, boys,' he said, 'but I guess I'm goin' to need it some more.'

'Anythin' we can do?' proffered the brothers unhesitatingly.

'Thanks,' answered Dan. 'I guess this trouble is shore goin' to flare up before long.'

'What's the next move?' asked Howard.

'We must hang on to those four hombres in there,' Dan replied with a nod in the direction of the cells, 'an' then we've got to make the charge stick.'

'We've got 'em cold with Jack's evidence,' pointed out Hoard.

'Shore, but we've got to keep Jack out of trouble.'

'You think they'll come gunnin' fer me?' asked Jack.

'Nothin' more likely,' drawled Dan, 'so here's what I figure we'll do. You an' Howard get out of town an'–'

'I'm not runnin' away,' protested Jack loudly.

'I'm not askin' you to,' went on Dan. 'I want you an' Howard to go up on to the bluffs overlookin' the Pickering spread an' report any movement from there. I reckon they'll try to break those four roughnecks out as well as get you.'

'Are you going to stop here, then?' asked Jack.

'I want someone fer the killin' of Mick Wilson. I know he's in the Broken U outfit an' I figure I know who. Clint's temporarily out of action so if your pa could come an' take over with a couple of more boys I'll get, then I'm after the killer.'

91

'Shore,' nodded the brothers. 'Pa'll be glad to help.'

The Collins brothers left the office and Dan settled down to await the arrival of their father. He was busy checking over the rifles which stood along one wall when the office door opened to admit Clint Schofield.

'Thought I told you to rest up fer a couple of days?' snapped Dan, but inwardly he was pleased to see the old deputy.

'Now don't git sore, Dan,' protested Clint. 'I heard you'd pulled in four of the Bar X outfit an' I figured this might bring a heap of trouble round your head before the night was out, so here I am.'

Dan grinned. 'An' mighty glad I am to see you, old timer.' He slapped Clint on the back in friendly greeting. 'Bill Collins is comin'; I guess I can leave these hombres in your care whilst I pull in the killer of Mick Wilson.'

Before Clint could reply the door opened and Bill Collins stepped in out of the darkness. Quickly Dan outlined his plans and left the office. He climbed into the saddle and turned for home.

Barbara had a meal ready, and not wanting to alarm her by his haste, he stayed and enjoyed it with her.

'I'm afraid I've got to go out to the Broken U, darlin', so don't wait up fer me,' said Dan.

'Must you go tonight, Dan? Can't it wait until morning?' pleaded Barbara.

Dan shook his head. ''Fraid not. I've got to get this thing settled.' He pushed himself out of his chair and picked up his Stetson little realising that the delay had saved him from a fruitless ride to the Broken U camp.

He kissed his wife lightly. 'Don't worry,' he murmured.

Barbara hid her fears and smiled bravely. 'All right, Dan,' she whispered. 'Be careful.'

As darkness settled over the Brazo River Matt Pickering paced the floor of the ranch-house, pulling hard at his cheroot.

'I don't like it, Luke,' he said. His voice was agitated. 'Those damn fools were care-less. Now thet word's out about the killin' Brooks'll git word to the other outfits along the trail.'

Luke lolled in a chair and smiled at his older brother. 'Ain't you fergittin' thet we hev the ford watched?'

Matt spun round. 'Be your age!' he snarled. 'You don't think a man like Brooks will let thet stop him. They'll not use it. There's plenty of places where a horse an' man can swim the Brazo an' we can't watch 'em all.'

'Wal, what you figure on doin'?' asked Luke spinning the chamber of his Colt.

Matt Pickering stopped in front of the fire and kicked the embers into a spluttering glow. He turned to face his brother.

'Guess we'll hev to do what we did last year when some of the herds used the southern ford – warn Gonzales!'

Luke stopped playing with his gun and sat up as if he had been stung.

'Now you're talkin' sense,' he said eagerly. 'Bigger stakes!'

'Yeah,' commented Matt doubtfully, 'an' more risk.'

'Aw, you're yellow,' said Luke in disgust.

Matt stiffened at his remark. 'You're hot headed an' it will run us into trouble yet, Luke. Be content with smaller takin's thet's safe, thet's what I always say, but now our hand's forced we'll go fer the bigger stuff. But don't fergit things got a bit hot fer Gonzales last year. Fortunately he was too much fer the law an' no one could connect us with him.'

'I think we can do without thet Mex,' spat Luke. 'I can run the show down there.'

'There you go again,' snarled Matt. 'Talk

sense. Gonzales knows the trails to an' over the border like the back of his hand, an' he knows where to git rid of the cattle. You try to do it an' it would be hopeless, besides, if you got the cattle over some Mex would slit your throat instead of buyin' the steers.' Matt pulled hard at his moustache and turned away in disgust. 'No, keep things as they are an' don't try to alter them.'

'All right, all right,' replied Luke. 'You're runnin' the show. I was only passin' opinions.'

'Wal, make sure you keep 'em as opinions,' answered Matt. 'I'll continue to run the show seein' it was my idea to git Wayman's spread in the first place.'

'Right, then what's the next move?' asked the fair-haired Luke.

'Send one of the boys to watch them herds an' when they turn south he rides hell-for-leather to contact Gonzales.'

'Yeah, but aren't you forgettin' one thing?' smirked Luke pleased with the thought that he had got one over on his brother.

'What's that?' asked Matt testily as he threw the cheroot stub into the fire.

'One of those four hombres in jail might talk an' they were all with us last year an' know about Gonzales.'

'I ain't forgotten that,' replied Matt icily. 'We're goin' to bust 'em out!'

'What! We'll never do it,' shouted Luke.

'Now who's yellow?' sneered Matt. ''Course we can do it, an' we'll do it tonight, it's dark enough now.' Matt picked up his gun belt and fastened it round his middle adding emphasis to his words. 'Send Red Murray over the Brazo to watch those herds, then git three of the boys an' come back here with them.'

Luke nodded and headed for the door.

'Luke,' called Matt to stop him. 'When we bust these four out they'd better git out of this area. You can ride with 'em an' take 'em to Gonzales an' link up with him.'

'Right,' nodded the tall, slim Kansan. 'What about McCoy in all this?'

'We'll deal with him if he crosses our path. If not then it'll be better fer him. He's got to find Mick Wilson's killer, an' thet Broken U outfit won't be easy to handle.'

Luke was soon back and five cowboys swung into their saddles and headed through the darkness for Red Springs.

Chapter 7

The Pickering brothers with their three side-kicks bunched behind rode steadily towards Red Springs.

Suddenly Matt put a steadying hand on Luke's reins and slowly pulled his own horse to a stop. The other riders milled around as they came alongside the two leading mounts.

'What's wrong?' called Luke puzzled by the halt.

Matt signalled him to keep quiet and then pointed over the grassland. Luke and the Bar X cowboys stared into the darkness, straining to see what had caused their leader to stop.

The fair-haired brother gasped when he saw the shadowy figures of a bunch of riders converging on the trail some distance ahead.

'Hold it, boys,' commanded Matt in a whisper. 'They haven't seen us yet.'

The Bar X cowpokes sat quietly on their horses watching the group ahead riding at a steady pace.

'Twenty of 'em,' whispered Luke.

Matt nodded. ''An they're comin' from the direction of the Broken U outfit.'

Luke drew a sharp breath. 'They shore are. Wonder what they're up to.'

'They're headin' for Red Springs so we'll soon know,' pointed out Matt.

The little group waited patiently for some signal from their leader. Matt narrowed his eyes, watching the shadows move against the night sky. They rode purposefully in a compact bunch significant of grim purpose. The riders swung on to the trail and only when they were barely discernible did Matt give the order to move. He matched his pace to that of the cowboys ahead and kept them just in sight.

The lights of Red Springs were showing across the darkened landscape when Matt noticed that the riders ahead slackened their pace.

'They're up to no good,' he whispered to Luke.

Luke nodded and checked the hang of his guns.

Matt called a halt outside the town but chose the position carefully so that he could keep the other outfit in sight. He was surprised when he saw them halt, dismount and hitch their horses at the first rail on Main Street.

'What they up to?' he muttered.

He frowned when he saw them bunch together and after a moment's pause spread out fanwise and walk slowly but purposefully along Main Street.

'Lynchin' party,' Matt hissed loudly.

'What!' Luke was startled as Matt's words hit him.

'If thet ain't a lynchin' party then I haven't seen one before,' muttered Matt, ''an they're after our men. They're gittin' townsfolk to join 'em. They'll be a howlin' mob by the time they reach the jail.'

Luke drew his Colt. 'C'm on,' he snapped. 'Let's bust 'em up.'

'Hold it, Luke,' Matt ordered.

Luke was stunned. 'What! We can't let 'em string up our boys.'

'We won't. This'll play right into our hands an' create the necessary diversion whilst we rescue Shorty an' the others,' grinned Matt.

The younger brother slipped his gun back into its holster. He smiled. 'I git it; the clever Mister Sheriff will be so taken up with thet mob thet he'll hev no time to devote to us.'

'Exactly,' laughed Matt. 'Let's ride.'

Dan McCoy turned his horse into Main Street. Startled by the sight of a mob hurrying along the dusty road he momentarily reined his horse to a stop but in a second spurred it into an urgent gallop. He flung himself from the saddle and leaped on to the boardwalk outside his office. He threw open the door shouting to Clint Schofield and Bill Collins.

'Quick, git the rifles,' he yelled.

He turned to face the mob who were some way down the street. Their shouts rose and fell as they called to others to join them. Beneath it was an angry murmuring of men whose reason was quickly leaving them.

Clint and Bill were beside Dan.

'Guessed this might happen,' muttered Clint gritting his teeth.

'Better give 'em a warning shot, Dan,' advised Collins emphasising his point by cocking his rifle.

'Wait,' said Dan. 'This'll maybe save me a ride to the Broken U camp. There's Brooks leadin' this party.'

Clint whistled between drawn lips. 'This isn't a break-out party, it's a lynchin' mob.'

Dan eased a Colt out of its holster. 'Keep near the doorway,' he ordered. 'If I fail git inside quick.'

Grim faced, his two friends shuffled back to the wall anxiously watching the yelling mob which hurried forward. Dan stepped forward to the edge of the sidewalk. He paused a moment, his face stern. He saw that the situation was going to need careful handling. Cowboys were swelling the crowd with every step it took. They knew nothing of the true situation but all that mattered to them was that a foul killing had taken place and someone should pay for it. This suited Brooks admirably for the bigger the crowd the easier it would be. His cowpokes yelled the news to every newcomer, sparing no detail and even adding to it.

'Hold it!' yelled Dan, striving to make himself heard above the angry cries of the cowpokes. He detected a hesitancy here and there but the Broken U riders did not falter and took with them the rest of the crowd. Dan shrugged his shoulders as if to move himself forward. He stepped from the sidewalk and walked three paces towards the mob.

'Hold it!' he shouted once more, but his words had no effect. His eyes hardened and his lips tightened in a grim line. As the yelling, gesticulating mob reached a pool of light spreading from the buildings on either side of the street, Dan's finger tightened on the trigger of his Colt. The bullet whined over the heads of the cowpokes. The mob stopped and the shouts died raggedly on the night air.

'The next will be lower if I hev to fire it,' warned Dan grimly.

'Git out of our way, McCoy,' snarled Brooks.

'You aimin' at takin' over?' asked Dan calmly.

'Figure on seein' justice done,' snapped the rancher.

Yells greeted this remark. 'String 'em up!' 'Murderin' coyotes.'

'Shut up!' Dan's voice lashed the crowd into silence. 'Half of you don't know what this is about so git yourselves away an' cool off.'

'We know those four men murdered Al Saunders,' spat Brooks, 'an' we figure on makin' 'em dance at the end of a rope.'

'Not while I'm here,' answered Dan coldly. 'They'll be tried in a legal manner.'

'They won't git a chance,' yelled Brooks. 'Come on, let's git 'em.' As he waved his arms the mob yelled its approval. Brooks took a step forward but a bullet at his feet stopped him in his tracks.

'I'm boss around here,' warned Dan grimly. 'One more step forward an' I'll clamp you in jail, Brooks. Jest the same as I'm takin' thet sidekick next to you fer the murder of Mick Wilson!'

The mob was stunned into silence. The local cowboys were shocked at the realisation that they had been following a murderer. Dan smiled grimly as some of the men on the fringe of the crowd started to shuffle away.

Brooks laughed harshly. 'Jeb Price? Don't be a fool, McCoy, you can't hold him.'

'You'll see,' replied Dan sternly. He stepped forward slowly but deliberately, his eyes alert knowing that the Broken U riders were itching to pull their Colts in defence of their comrade. Dan stopped in front of the mob. Without a word he pulled Jeb's gun from its holster and flung it into the dust. His hand flashed up, grabbed the cowpoke's shirt and with a strong pull sent him sprawling towards the sidewalk.

'Take him, Clint,' Dan shouted over his shoulder, and slowly backed away from the crowd.

An angry murmur ran through the Broken U cowboys. Brooks, his eyes blazing with fury, moved his hand towards his gun.

'Don't do thet!' warned Dan.

'You can't hold him,' yelled Burrows furiously.

'I hev witnesses!' answered Dan.

'You haven't, there was no one about.' Anger filled Burrows as he saw his buddy held prisoner by Clint Schofield and Bill Collins.

'Thanks,' laughed Dan harshly, 'thet tells me thet Price did it.'

'Fool,' lashed Brooks at his rider. 'Can't you ever keep your mouth shut?'

Dan stepped on to the sidewalk and paused. 'Now, if you townsfolk still feel like followin' Brooks there's another murderer you'll hev to take as well.'

The crowd began to disperse, groups murmuring amongst themselves, but the Broken U men stood firm. Before Brooks could reply the sound of fast ridden horses sounded along the street. All heads turned to stare at two riders who raised the dust. Howard and Jack Collins pulled their horses to a sliding stop before the sheriff's office.

'The Pickerings left the Bar X,' shouted Jack breathlessly.

'Headin' fer Red Springs when we last saw 'em,' panted Howard.

'What's this all about?' yelled Brooks.

'I anticipated trouble from the Pickerings, not from you,' replied Dan curtly. 'Bill,' he called over his shoulder, 'go through an' watch the back. We haven't seen 'em here,' continued Dan, 'guess you're away ahead of 'em.'

'Couldn't be,' said Jack a puzzled frown creasing his forehead. 'We lost 'em in the dark an'—'

His words were cut short as his father burst through the office door yelling at the top of his voice. 'Dan! They're gone!'

Dan spun on his heel. 'What!' he gasped.

'Broke out of the window,' said Collins.

'Now ain't we got a clever Mister Sheriff,' burst in Brooks furiously.

'An' if you hadn't been causin' a breach of the peace with this mob I could have had my eyes on the prisoners. As it is the Pickerings used you as a diversion an' helped themselves.' Anger flushed Dan's face. His eyes blazed with fury as he faced Brooks. 'Now git, an' let me handle this.' He swung round and strode into his office.

Chapter 8

Dan rushed to the cells. The bars on the windows had been ripped out of their sockets giving the prisoners an easy means of escape. Followed by Howard and Jack Collins the sheriff hurried out of the back door of the building and examined the marks below the windows.

'It's difficult to see in this light, but they hadn't any horses here,' Dan informed his companions. 'They made off thet way an' must have left their horses on the south side of the town.' Dan did not hesitate any longer. 'C'm on,' he shouted, 'we'll try a long shot.'

He raced round the corner with Howard and Jack close on his heels. The Broken U outfit had disappeared from the street and Dan guessed they were on their way back to their camp. Little knots of people still hung about and they looked up sharply as Dan clattered across the boards. He flung open the office door and yelled inside.

'Clint! We're ridin'. You an' Bill keep your eye on thet hombre in there, don't let him be sprung.'

The deputy's words were lost to Dan as he jumped from the sidewalk and leaped into the saddle alongside the Collins brothers who were already turning their mounts. As one, the three friends kicked their horses forward and with hoofs pounding the hard dusty road left town by the south road. After riding about half a mile away from the buildings Dan pulled off the trail to a smaller rise where he drew to a halt.

Leaving Howard with the horses Dan and Jack hurried to the top of the rise. Straining their eyes to pierce the darkness they lay flat to keep watch.

'I figure they may hold back in town until things quieten down an' then slip out,' said Dan.

'Do you reckon they'll go back to the Bar X?' questioned Jack.

'No, at least not the four hombres we want. We've nothin' on anyone else an' we don't even know if it was the Pickerings that got them out of jail.'

'But who else could it be?' gasped Jack.

'No one,' replied Dan, 'but we can't prove it.'

'Wal, there's no sign of any riders,' said Jack, 'not even the Broken U; they must have ridden hard.'

'I guess they're anxious to git back,' drawled Dan. 'They'll be movin' in the mornin' otherwise they'll hold up other herds when they reach the ford.'

'Can't we pick up this trail in daylight?' asked Jack.

'Shore,' nodded Dan tipping his sombrero back with his thumb, 'if there's one to find then.'

Jack looked sharply at the sheriff. Dan smiled.

'They'll be smart enough not to leave one,' he added.

The conversation lagged as the two cowboys patiently kept watch. The night darkened. Dan stirred uneasily. It was going to be difficult to pick anyone out unless they rode close by. Suddenly Dan stiffened. A flicker of light flared in the darkness towards the Brazo and then was gone. Dan gripped Jack's arm.

'See that?' he whispered.

'Yeah, seems to be down by the Bar X,' answered Jack. 'I wonder if–'

His words were cut short with a gasp when he saw the light flicker, flare and shoot skywards.

'Fire at the Bar X!' yelled Dan. 'C'm on!'

He jumped to his feet and sent stones and earth flying before him as he slid down the hillside closely followed by Jack. The horses, alarmed at the noise, were held steady by Howard who was already in the saddle when Dan and Jack swung on to their mounts.

'Bar X's on fire,' called Dan wheeling his black round and kicking it into a gallop. The two brothers were close on the heels of the powerful horse and earth and grass flew as the three cowboys urged their horses towards the Brazo which now reflected the flames engulfing the Bar X buildings.

Dan's face was grim as he raced towards the inferno. He swore he would have Brooks in jail before daylight if he found that this was his doing. Flames leaped high and sparks showered skywards amidst rolling black smoke as the fire took command and gripped the house and neighbouring buildings in its devouring heat.

The three men hauled their sweating horses to a halt some distance from the inferno. They leaped from the saddles and sprinted towards the fire. They could detect no sign of life, only the flames danced casting their ever-changing light over the ground.

'Doesn't appear to be anyone here,'

shouted Jack above the roar of burning timber.

'Over there,' yelled Howard and sprinted towards a figure sprawled on the ground. He dropped beside the still cowboy and turned him over. Blood oozed from his chest.

'Dead,' said Howard grimly as he rose to his feet.

The sheriff turned towards the fire. Its macabre light showed another prone figure and Dan hurried forward. He had no need to examine the man carefully; a bullet had split his head open.

A sudden, wild, frightened whinny shook the air. Dan was startled. He leaped over the body and ran towards the stables. Flames were licking one end of the building and were starting their devouring run along the timbers. By the time the three men reached the doorway half the building was a raging inferno. So intent were they on reaching the animals that they almost fell over the cow-‧ boy who lay half way through the door. A moan took Jack on to his knee beside the man.

'Get him out,' yelled Dan above the screams and cries of the frightened horses.

The animals kicked in their stalls struggling to free themselves to escape from the burning terror. Dan leaped forward pulling his knife from his belt. Hoofs flashed in the flames, kicking at the air in an attempt to escape from death but prevented their would-be rescuer from reaching the ropes which tied them to their stalls.

A loud crash from the end of the stable as a huge beam fell to the ground silenced the terrified cries of two of the horses. Sparks showered everywhere and Dan recoiled momentarily as the heat intensified. He looked round desperately. If only he could reach the beam half way up the wall to which the horses were tied. He glanced upwards and leaped to grasp a cross-beam and pull himself up. Already sparks were settling on the timber threatening to ignite it, but without hesitation Dan bent double and moved swiftly towards the wall. Quickly he lowered himself on to the other beam and crawled to the first horse. Its eyes wide with terror the animal pulled frantically at the rope. Dan leaned downwards and with a swift slash severed the rope. The horse backed and twisted free of the stall and snorting loudly galloped from the blazing stables.

Dan scrambled quickly along the beam

and cut the other horses free. Flames leaped high. Dan felt them singeing his face and hands. Smoke choked his throat as he gasped for air. He dropped into the stall vacated by the last horse and holding his forearms across his face half staggered and half ran for the door. He hesitated for a moment when he saw that the doorway now presented a frame of flames. Summoning his strength, which seemed to have suddenly drained by the effort in the heat and smoke, he stumbled blindly from the inferno, retching and coughing.

Howard raced to the blazing stables, caught him in his arms and led him to Jack and the wounded cowboy. Dan flopped on the ground his lungs drinking in the cool, soothing, reviving air. He was only dully aware of the three figures close to him but gradually his senses cleared and he welcomed the cool water which moistened his parched lips.

Feeling better, Dan sat up and gazed at the buildings engulfed in flames.

'You nearly didn't git out of there,' said Howard.

Dan smiled wryly. 'I couldn't see the poor beasts burn,' he muttered. 'How is he?' he asked nodding towards the wounded man.

'Pretty bad,' whispered Jack.

'Said anythin'?' asked Dan.

'Lot of mumblin' thet I can't make out.'

A groan brought them quickly to their knees beside the figure stretched on the ground. Dan gently raised the man's head.

'A drink,' said Dan, and Jack held his Stetson towards the cowboy.

The flames cast a dancing light across the rugged face drawn in pain. The water brought a flicker of reason from the man. His eyes stared upwards, wide and frightened.

'Who did it?' asked Dan quietly. He repeated the question again and slowly the man's eyes moved until they focused on the three men beside him.

'We're friends,' whispered Dan. 'Who attacked you?'

The man's lips trembled in their effort to speak. It seemed eternity before the first word was forced out.

'Three – Broken – U.' The words came in gasps. 'Never had – a chance. Got – Sam an' Butch – before we–' The voice trailed away, the lips still moving. '–ran to – stables – plugged me–'

'All right, take it easy,' said Dan soothingly. 'We'll git the killers.'

The wounded man stiffened. His eyes widened in a terrifying stare. 'Broken U. Broken U, three, only three–' The words croaking from his lips stopped suddenly, his head fell to one side and his body crumpled.

Dan lay the body down gently. He straightened himself with a long sigh. Suddenly he spun on his heel and with a curt 'C'm on,' ran towards the horses. He leaped into the saddle and pulled the black round, closely followed by the Collins' brothers.

The sheriff urged his horse into a gallop. Jack and Howard followed suit and drew alongside Dan. They did not query his action but guessed he was heading for the Broken U camp. The powerful animals flew across the ground and soon the camp fires twinkling in the hollow came in sight.

The sound of hard ridden horses brought the Broken U riders to their feet around their boss and when Dan and the Collins boys hit camp they were faced with drawn Colts. They hauled their horses to a stop in front of the group.

'You won't need them,' yelled Dan and saw the guns slipped back into their holsters on a nod from Brooks.

'Got the jail breakers, Sheriff?' asked Brooks as Dan swung from the saddle.

'No,' replied the sheriff. 'I'm here about thet.' He nodded over his shoulder in the direction of the fire which appeared as a glow in the sky over the ridge around the hollow.

'Thet?' puzzled Brooks.

'Yes.'

'What is it?'

'Bar X.'

'Bar X!' Brooks gasped, and a murmur ran through the cowboys. 'What happened?'

Dan was puzzled. The cattleman's surprise seemed genuine enough and he thought he detected a look of horror in the older man's face. Had the Bar X cowboy been wrong?

'Brooks, quick, check your herders,' snapped Dan.

A puzzled frown furrowed the rancher's forehead. His eyes narrowed.

'What you gettin' at?' he asked quietly.

'Three Bar X hands were murdered out there an' the whole place fired. One cowpoke died in my arms testifyin' thet three of your boys did it.'

'What!' Brooks exploded. 'He's been out of his head. We came straight back here from Red Springs.'

'Thet may be. I followed a hunch thet who ever did it stopped to watch his handiwork somewhere on the way back. If any of your cowpokes are missin' then I've got my men.'

Brooks drew a sharp breath. 'Check, Red,' he ordered curtly.

Dan saw that the rancher was fighting hard to control his feelings, but whether it was anger at being found out or anger because his men had run foul of the law over something he knew nothing about Dan could only guess at the moment.

Red was back in a few minutes. His grim face told the result before he announced, 'Three missin' boss.'

Brook's face darkened; his eyes blazed. 'Who are they?' he snapped through clenched teeth.

'Sol Myers, Tay Edwards and Kid Denvers,' replied the foreman grimly.

Brooks swung round to face Dan. 'Sheriff,' he said quietly, 'I'll swear I knew nothin' about this.'

There was an unmistakable sincerity in his voice and Dan knew that Brooks was telling the truth. The man before him suddenly looked weary. Dan did not speak; he sensed that the older man had more to say.

'Those three hoodlums aren't regular riders of mine. They rode with Jed Burrows and Jeb Price. I've hired 'em before; there's a streak of trouble makin' in 'em but I've handled 'em other times.' The rancher paused. A note of sadness crept into his voice. 'Maybe I'm slippin'.'

A scuffle on the edge of the gathering cut short the conversation. Suddenly a cowboy was sent sprawling in front of Brooks and the sheriff. Howard stepped forward.

'Caught him sneakin' off.'

'All right, Burrows, git on your feet,' snapped Dan. 'You won't be warning your friends.'

'Take him in hand fer the sheriff, Red,' ordered Brooks.

The foreman nodded and pushed Burrows forward roughly.

'I don't git this, Brooks,' said Dan. 'You hotly defended Price earlier this evenin'.'

'Look, Sheriff, I'm boss an' I'll defend my riders within reason. I knew nothin' of the killin' of Mick Wilson. I've learned since thet it was a personal matter – somethin' happened between him an' Jeb when we crossed the ford. Thet led to the murder of Al Saunders an' thet made me hoppin' mad comin' on top of the toll. I may be tough an' will fight fer what's right, but I wouldn't sink as low as firin' a man's property.' His voice paused and before he could speak

Dan's hand gripped his arm to silence him.

A tense quietness hung over the circle of men as they listened to the clop of horses' hoofs and the raucous laughter of the riders. The dancing light from the fire picked out three horsemen as they emerged from the darkness. Their gaiety suddenly left them when they saw the silent circle of men.

The centre rider forced a laugh as they swung from the saddles. 'Wal, boss, you'll hev no more trouble from the Pickerings; they'll be far too busy, won't they boys?'

His sidekicks laughed as they affirmed his remark.

Dan glanced at Brooks and saw a man ablaze with anger. The rancher stepped forward and as Howard was about to stop him Dan whispered, 'Let Brooks deal with this.'

'You low down, good-fer-nothin' hoodlums,' Brooks hissed. 'You were told not to leave the camp tonight and–'

'But we've fixed the Pickerings fer you,' gasped one of the cowboys amazed at Brooks's reaction.

'I'll fight, an' fight tough but never the way you've done.' The rancher's voice lashed the three men before him with contempt. 'I've hed my ranch fired an' seen the agony of trapped horses. Don't expect you

118

gave 'em a thought.'

'Why should we?' said one of the cowboys toughening up to the rancher's attitude. 'They was Pickering's horses.'

Brooks could contain himself no longer. He leaped forward and smashed his fist into the cowpuncher's face. The cowboy reeled backwards and fell sprawling on the hard ground. Brooks stood over him, his eyes blazing with anger.

'You're fer the sheriff,' he yelled.

The three killers went for their guns, snarling like cornered animals, but Dan and the Collins boys were faster. Colts roared and stabbed the darkness with their flashes. Two cowboys died before they could pull the trigger, but the third loosed off a shot as he crumpled on the ground. With a yell of pain Brooks spun round and staggered backwards as the bullet crashed into his thigh. Dan and the Broken U foreman leaped to his side and caught him before he fell. Supporting him in their powerful arms they laid him down gently close to the fire.

The rancher's face twisted with pain as Dan examined the wound. 'Better git him to town quick,' instructed Dan to the foreman.

Red nodded and ordered two of his cowpunchers to get ready.

Dan turned to Brooks. 'It isn't too bad if the Doc sees it quick, but it'll probably lay you up fer a week or two.'

'Can't, got to see these herds through,' gasped Brooks.

'I guess Red can handle things,' answered Dan.

Brooks relaxed and breathed deeply. 'Shore, he can,' he nodded. 'Keep 'em movin', Red, an' watch out fer Pickering. Guess he'll be plenty sore when he sees thet ranch after the fire. Reckon he'll take it out of the herds headin' this way, especially mine; good job we're sendin' 'em south.'

'Don't worry about anythin' boss, I'll see everythin's all right,' assured Red. He did not speak again until the rancher had disappeared into the darkness in the direction of Red Springs. 'Where do you figure the Pickering outfit headed?' he asked the sheriff.

Dan eased the sombrero on his head. 'Don't know,' he said thoughtfully. 'I figured they might hev hid in town fer a short while, but I reckon I was wrong or they'd hev seen the fire. They must hev ridden hard, but where they headed thet's another guess.'

Chapter 9

Matt Pickering flattened on his horse's back as the Bar X riders pounded away from Red Springs. The jail-break had been easy: with the sheriff's attention diverted by the Broken U bunch the bars on the window had been wrenched from their sockets enabling the prisoners to squeeze into the freedom of the night. They had crept quickly but stealthily away from the jail and all that remained was to get as far away from the town as possible before the escape was discovered.

His brother, Luke, was puzzled by Matt's prolonged gallop. He had expected Matt to call a halt, split forces and return to the ranch whilst he and the four cowpokes they had broken out of jail went south to join Gonzales.

They covered the miles rapidly and as the trail dipped Red Springs and the surrounding countryside was soon out of sight. Everyone held the thought of possible pursuit and many a backward glance was cast as the miles pounded by. Eventually Matt left the trail and headed to some thickets close to the Brazo, where he called a halt.

'Guess we can wait here until daylight,' said the dark, moustached leader as he slipped from his horse. 'Git all the rest you can, there's a long ride ahead tomorrow.'

'Aren't you goin' back?' asked Luke as he tied his horse to the branch of a tree.

'Shore, in the morning,' answered Matt. 'We'll stay with you in case by some chance thet nosey sheriff's gotten on to our trail.'

Luke eased the saddle from his horse. 'I can handle him,' he bragged.

'An' supposin' he brings a posse?' asked Matt. 'No, we'll stay jest in case.'

Guards were posted but the night was uneventful and the next morning the party split up. Matt watched his brother and the four jail-birds out of sight before he called the other Bar X riders into the saddle and headed for the ranch.

They rode at a leisurely pace, laughing and joking about the way they had out-witted the sheriff. As they crested a rise the smile vanished from Matt's face and words died on his lips. He recoiled with shock at what he saw and automatically hauled his horse to a stop. Around him the Bar X cowboys pulled up sharply, their eyes wide with amazement and horror at the scene which lay below them at the foot of the hill.

Matt gritted his teeth: a long slow breath escaped from his tightened lips. His eyes narrowed and he cursed loudly.

'What's happened?' he snarled as he gazed upon the black smouldering ruins of his ranch. 'C'm on, let's find out,' he yelled, kicking his horse forward.

The chestnut stretched itself answering its rider's urging. Earth flew as it flashed down the hillside closely followed by the grim-faced Bar X riders.

Matt's eyes blazed with fury as he raced towards the burnt-out buildings. The cowboys looked in vain for some sign of life but the only movement came from the wisps of smoke which curled lazily on the still air.

Reaching the blackened remains of the ranch the cowpokes pulled their mounts to a dust-raising sliding halt.

'Over there, boss,' yelled a chiselled-face rider pointing in the direction of the huddled bodies of the ranch-hands.

They pushed their horses forward. Matt was the first to reach the still figures and was soon on his knees beside them. Slowly he straightened, his face black with anger. His knuckles showed white as he clenched his fists, fighting to control the fury which mounted within him.

'Shot before they hed a chance to draw,' he hissed. He turned to the two cowboys beside him. 'See to the bodies,' he muttered and walked slowly away.

A cowboy hurried from the burnt-out stables. 'Some of the horses got out,' he panted as he reached his boss. 'But three poor devils hadn't a chance in there.'

Matt looked up sharply. 'I don't get it. Things don't quite add up. How could they get out?'

'You don't think it was hoss thieves?' asked the cowpoke.

'Hoss thieves would hev taken the lot, besides, I don't figure they'd hev fired the place.' His eyes narrowed but they blazed with anger. 'This was done to hit me hard an' I reckon Brooks'll know somethin' about it. C'm on, we'll tear the Broken U apart if necessary.'

He ran to his horse and leaped into the saddle, turning the animal as he did so. The Bar X riders quickly followed their boss, leaving behind two of their number to perform the last duty for their dead partners.

Horses streaked across the ground as they were urged faster and faster by their riders.

Brooks's name pounded in Matt's brain until all reason was driven out. He gave no thought to any plan of surprise attack, only wanting to come face to face with Brooks as soon as possible. Eager to be in the Broken U camp Matt Pickering did not slacken the pace as they raced towards the edge of the hollow over which they would ride into the camp.

Suddenly he half checked the horse with surprise as three figures rose above the rim of the hollow and stood in the path of the riders. He frowned grimly, gave the horse its head and pounded towards the three men. He was determined to ride straight over them, until a shot from each of them roared over the heads of the horsemen. The riders hauled on the reins and the horses, snorting and tossing their heads against the pull of the leather slid to a halt facing the sheriff and the Collins brothers.

'Out of my way, Sheriff!' yelled Pickering angrily. He glared hatred at Dan as he pulled on the reins to keep his horse steady. 'I've a score to settle with Brooks.'

'Been expectin' you, Pickering,' answered Dan calmly. 'You two aren't gettin' near each other if I can help it.'

Pickering's face darkened. He leaned forward, his eyes narrowing as he glared at Dan.

'I'll kill thet two-bit Texan,' he hissed. He flung his arm, pointing in the direction of the Bar X. 'You should see my ranch back there.'

'I have,' said Dan casually.

Pickering straightened in the saddle, his eyes widening at this surprise announcement.

'What!' Pickering gasped. 'Then why aren't you doin' somethin' about it?'

'Nothin' I could do when I got there except let a few horses loose,' replied Dan. 'The place was a roarin' inferno.'

Pickering's eyes softened a little. 'So thet's why some of the horses weren't in the stable. Many thanks, Sheriff.' He paused a moment as he caught his breath. 'But thet isn't bringin' my men back. What you goin' to do about thet?'

'It's been done,' answered Dan, 'so git your bunch out of here.'

The horseman's eyes narrowed. He leaned forward in the saddle, staring straight at Dan. 'See here, McCoy, I'm not leavin' here until I've seen Brooks. I've no quarrel with you so git out of my way. If you don't I'm comin' straight through you.' He straightened in the saddle and glanced round at his riders who were ranged alongside him, grim-faced as they awaited his signal. Pickering turned back to McCoy in time to see him raise his hand.

At this sign the Broken U cowboys with guns covering the riders slowly revealed themselves from behind the rim of the hollow.

Pickering's lips narrowed grimly as he drew a sharp breath. His eyes blazed with fury at Dan as he cursed loudly.

'Might hev known you'd side with this bunch of murderin' Texans.'

'I ain't sidin' with them; jest stopping you from doing something that doesn't need doing,' replied Dan.

'Three of my men lay dead back there,' yelled Pickering scowling angrily, 'and my buildings have been burnt to the ground; you've seen 'em and all you can say is that nothing needs doing about it. Wal, I'm telling you, McCoy, I'm coming clean through you.'

Dan saw Pickering tense himself in the saddle. He stepped forward quickly, menacing the rider with his Colt.

'Hold it, Pickering.' Dan's words and attitude left no doubt in the rider's mind as to what would happen if he scraped his spurs against his horse.

'What needed doin' has been done,' finished Dan.

'What do you mean?' asked the Kansan doubtfully.

'Brooks had nothin' to do with this,' replied the sheriff. 'He knew nothin' about it until I rode in with the news.'

He was interrupted with a loud unbelieving laugh. 'There's no one else around here thet hed do it but the Broken U,' spat Pickering.

'Yeah, they were Broken U riders right enough, one of your men told me just before he died.'

A murmur ran through the riders and Dan was interrupted by their shouts.

'Then what you protectin' 'em for?' snarled Pickering.

'I ain't. I came here to get 'em an' now they lie buried on yon hillside. Brooks got wounded in the gunplay an' he's in town.'

Matt eyed the sheriff suspiciously. 'You sure?' he quizzed.

'If you don't believe me then take a ride over there an' see fer yourself,' answered Dan.

'Guess I will at that,' said Pickering pushing his horse forward.

A tense silence gripped the two opposing groups of cow-punchers as Pickering rode quickly across the hollow and up the hillside above the Broken U camp. The waiting men saw him pause before turning his horse back towards them.

'Wal?' asked Dan as Pickering rode slowly up to them. 'Satisfied?'

Pickering grunted contemptuously. 'You may have started to do your job, Sheriff, but it doesn't pay me fer my losses. If Brooks can't control his cowpokes then he's responsible in my eyes.' He leaned forward in his saddle emphasising each word. 'An' he's goin' to pay.'

Dan's eyes narrowed as he faced the rancher. 'Pickering, I'm warning you, don't interfere with this herd nor the one thet's comin' up the trail or else there'll be a heap of trouble for you.'

'You can't stop me, Sheriff, so save your breath.'

Before Pickering could ride forward Dan seized the stirrup. He looked up at the dark, moustached face.

'There'll be no more warnings,' said Dan grimly. 'By the way, there were only three of your cowpokes at the ranch. Where were the rest of you?'

'We hed somethin' to see to,' replied Pickering curtly.

'Would thet be bustin' your sidekicks out of jail?' rapped Dan.

Matt smirked. 'Don't tell me you let 'em git away, Sheriff.' An incredulous look crossed his face and his riders laughed loudly.

Dan's eyes narrowed angrily. 'I guess you know they did but–'

'You can't prove it,' mocked Pickering finishing Dan's sentence for him.

The young cowboy ignored this remark. His eyes flashed across the bunch of horsemen. 'I see brother Luke isn't with you. Where is he?'

'Out ridin',' retorted Matt.

'With jail-birds?' rasped Dan.

Pickering looked hard at Dan. 'Keep your nose out of this, Sheriff, or thet pretty wife of yours may soon be a widow.'

He stabbed his horse with his spurs and the animal leaped forward. The Bar X cowboys wheeled their horses and quickly followed their boss. Silently Dan watched the whirling cloud of dust which marked their progress towards the Brazo.

Suddenly he turned to the Broken U foreman. 'Wal, Red,' he said, 'I guess you can roll now. You won't hev any more trouble from Pickering, but I wouldn't say as much fer your second herd.'

Red nodded his agreement and yelled orders which sent the Broken U men hurrying to their camp. Swiftly but skilfully the trail-riders set about their tasks eager to be on their way to the railhead. Dan took leave of the foreman and after thanking the cowboy who had been guarding Jed Burrows he motioned the prisoner towards the horses.

'C'm on, Burrows, you're goin' to join Jeb behind bars as an accomplice to the murder of Mick Wilson and old Silas.'

Burrows did not answer but his face burned black with hate for the sheriff. Slowly he walked towards his horse, his shifty eyes seeking some means of escape. Suddenly as they passed one of the trail herders, Burrows moved swiftly sideways, jerking the Colt from the man's holster. He spun round, crouching like some wild animal making a desperate defence to save its life. His finger squeezed the trigger but Dan was quicker. He dived forward, a gun leaping like lightning to his hand. Before Dan hit the ground lead crashed into Burrows, grinding him to the dust.

Chapter 10

Through the following days Dan scoured the countryside for trace of the escaped murderers, but they had vanished completely. For a week a close watch was kept on the Bar X where Matt Pickering salvaged the ruins and erected temporary buildings to serve as shelter, but not once was there any communication between Matt and his brother, Luke.

'I don't like it,' said Dan pushing his sombrero to the back of his head as he flopped into his office chair. 'Somethin' brewin'; I can feel it.'

'You're too suspicious, Sheriff,' laughed Brooks, now almost recovered from his wound. 'I put paid to Pickering's party when I got the other herders to turn south and use the southern ford across the Brazo.'

'Thet's jest what I don't like,' puzzled Dan. 'Pickering's taken it too calmly.'

'Maybe he knows when he's licked,' commented Clint rubbing his stubbled chin. 'I guess the Crooked Z will be well to the south now.'

'An' my second bunch won't be far behind,' said Brooks as he rolled himself a cigarette.

'You fergit, Pickering threatened revenge after his place was burnt down,' drawled Dan. 'An' Pickering ain't likely to fergit in a hurry.'

'What can he do?' asked Brooks smoothing the cigarette between his fingers. 'He's beaten an' knows it.'

Dan pushed himself from his chair and strode slowly to the window. 'Then why hasn't Luke Pickering returned to help his brother? Why should he ride with jail-birds?'

'Maybe he isn't with 'em; maybe he got wise an' saw the game was up,' Brooks pointed out.

'You forget thet he'd gone before we knew thet the herds had definitely turned south.'

'Yeah, but he knew Brooks was goin' to try to persuade them to do so,' said Clint.

'Shore, he must have had a high regard fer my persuasive powers,' grinned the rancher.

Dan did not answer but continued to stare out of the window. Suddenly he stiffened.

'This smells of trouble,' he flung over his shoulder.

Clint and Brooks were by his side in a flash, to see a dust-covered, hatless cowboy hitting town as if the devil pursued him.

'A cowpoke without his sombrero spells trouble,' muttered Dan as he pushed past the others and rushed to the door. He flung it open and strode on to the sidewalk with Clint and Brooks close behind him.

The rider, his clothes torn and caked with dust, hurled himself from his horse and stumbled up the steps to the sheriff. His knees began to buckle under him and Dan jumped forward to catch him before he fell.

'Clint, quick,' Dan called.

The deputy grasped the rider by his left arm and gently took some of the weight from Dan.

'He's hurt bad,' said Dan indicating the right arm covered in blood from an ugly wound near the shoulder. 'Git him into the office.'

The cowboy gasped for breath, his eyes wide with question and hope. 'You the sheriff?' he panted.

'Yeah,' answered Dan.

Relief crossed the rider's face as he expelled a sigh of satisfaction. Suddenly he stiffened, struggling to stand. As he turned to Dan the sheriff saw the relief turn to concern.

'You must ride,' he gasped. 'Git those murderin' coyotes, they–' He shuddered and his voice trailed away.

'Take it easy son, take it easy,' comforted Dan. 'Tell me later.'

A small crowd had gathered and Jack and Howard Collins pushed their way through.

'Jack,' called Dan as the brothers mounted the steps, 'git the Doc, quick.'

Jack nodded and hurried across the boards, his feet beating an urgent tattoo.

Dan and Clint carried the cowboy into the office and gently lowered him into a chair. Howard pressed a drink to the wounded man's lips. He shuddered as the liquid stirred some life and he struggled to sit upright in the chair.

'Steady, son,' said Dan gently. 'The Doc will soon hev you patched up.'

The cowboy's eyes focused on the star on Dan's shirt. He nodded weakly as he looked into the reassuring eyes of the sheriff.

'I made it,' he muttered and sank back with a sign of relief.

Howard pressed another drink to the man's lips. He coughed, shuddered and doubled forward wincing with pain as he became aware of his shattered shoulder. He looked up at Dan.

'They wiped us out,' he whispered. 'I'm

135

the only one who got away; guess they thought they'd got me.'

Alarm showed on Dan's face as he glanced sharply at his companions.

'Who you talkin' about?' he asked anxiously.

The cowboy reached for another drink. Another spasm of coughing followed.

'All right, son,' comforted Dan, 'never mind my questions now. The Doc will soon be here an' you can talk when he's fixed you up.'

Hurried footsteps sounded on the boards and the door was flung open to admit the doctor and Jack Collins. The doctor nodded to Dan, put his brown hat and black bag on the table, and without a word quickly examined the stranger.

'Your arm's in a bad way, son,' he said, 'but you'll be all right – we'll soon have you patched up.'

The doctor turned to the men who stood anxiously watching the proceedings. The orders which he issued were obeyed quickly and precisely and not a word was spoken by anyone but the doctor as he worked quickly and methodically cutting away the blood-stained shirt and cleaning the ugly wound.

When he was satisfied he turned to his bag

on the table and with a slight inclination of his head called Dan over to him.

'I'm goin' to have to get the lead out of thet arm,' he whispered as he fumbled inside the bag for his implements. 'That's goin' to hurt some. I want you to hang on to his arms.'

Dan nodded and moved behind the cowboy in the chair. As the doctor leaned over the wound Dan gripped the stranger tightly. The wounded man's face twisted in pain as the doctor probed inside the gaping hole for the bullet. He stifled a cry, biting his lip deep so that the blood flowed; beads of sweat broke on his face and ran from his forehead; his legs jerked and Howard and Jack jumped forward to grip them tightly; his head twitched in agony until the pain became so unbearable that he fainted.

The doctor glanced anxiously at the face, deathly white with torture. Suddenly with a triumphant grunt he straightened, jerked his wrist and extracted the bullet.

The tension in the office eased as everyone relaxed. Leather-faced old Clint blew out his cheeks and wiped the back of his hand across his forehead.

'I shore never want to see thet again,' he muttered turning to the window.

'Will he be all right?' asked Dan.

'Sure,' answered the doctor briefly, preparing the dressing for the wound. 'Mind you,' he added, 'he's lost a lot of blood and his exhausted condition has left him very weak. He needs someone to look after him.'

'All right, Doc, I'll fix it,' said Dan. 'Babs won't mind fer a few days.'

'Good,' replied the doctor turning to the wounded man. 'He'll be in good hands.'

He dressed the wound swiftly and a few minutes later straightened himself with a sigh of satisfaction.

'He'll be all right now,' he said with a smile. He started to pack his bag. 'Who is he, Dan?'

'Don't know,' answered the sheriff with a puzzled shake of his head. 'Thet's what I want to know. Muttered somethin' about bein' the only survivor, but where he's from I don't know.'

'Wal, don't question him fer long when he comes round,' instructed the doctor picking up his hat. 'I'll be round to see him to-morrow.'

Dan nodded. 'Thanks, Doc,' he said.

As the door shut Dan glanced anxiously at the white-faced cowboy who showed no sign of stirring.

The sheriff paced the floor restlessly, casting anxious glances at the wounded man. It seemed like eternity before the cowboy moved, but it was no more than five minutes.

A groan made Dan spin on his heels and leap to the man's side. The others jumped at the sound, sprang from their chairs or pushed themselves away from the window to gather round in eager anticipation of his news.

Dan grabbed a mug and held a drink to the man's lips. He sipped eagerly. Slowly his eyes cleared and he looked round the faces staring at him.

'Sorry I passed out,' he said with an apologetic smile.

'Best thing thet could hev happened,' reassured Dan. 'Doc's patched you up but says you must rest fer awhile. I'll take you home; my wife will see that you get well quickly.'

The cowboy muttered his thanks as he pushed himself into a more comfortable position in the chair.

'Think you can manage to tell us your story now?' asked Dan.

'Yeah, I reckon so,' he nodded. He reached for the mug and took another drink before continuing. 'My name's Wes Bridges an' I ride for the Crooked Z.' He paused and bit his lip. 'Thet should be *rode* fer the Crooked Z; they jest don't exist any more thanks to thet low down coyote Brooks of the Broken U!'

The circle of men glanced in amazement at one another. Dan looked sharply at Brooks who was so astonished he could not speak. Dan leaned forward quickly.

'What do you mean, Wes?' he asked.

'We got word from Brooks not to use Wayman's Ford but to go south. We–'

Brooks had recovered from his surprise and interrupted Bridges to confirm this last announcement. 'Thet's right,' he said. 'I'm Brooks an'–'

Anger flared in the cowboy's face. Surprise, at being confronted by the man he was condemning, mixed with hate, as he tried to push himself out of the chair. 'You low-down scurvy coyote,' he yelled.

'Easy, son,' said Dan quickly, holding Bridges back in the chair. 'What are you getting' at?' He held his hand to quieten Brooks who was about to speak.

'Him,' replied Wes angrily, nodding at Brooks. 'Pulled a fast one; sent us south an' then jumped us; wiped out the Crooked Z an' rustled all the cattle.'

'Why should I do thet?' stormed Brooks startled by the accusations.

'Your spread borders on the Crooked Z, could be you'd like the lot,' spat Bridges.

'Why, you – you,' spluttered Brooks trying to find the words he wanted. He turned to Dan. 'Sheriff, you tell him; you know it was impossible for me to do what he says.'

Dan looked quizzingly at Brooks. His lips tightened in a wry smile as he raised his eyebrows. 'Is it?' he asked. 'It's a possibility I hadn't thought of an' knowin' what I know extremely unlikely.' He grinned at the relief which flooded the rancher's face to replace the look of annoyance at his first words. Dan turned to Bridges. 'How do you know they were Broken U riders thet jumped you?'

'Wal, they–' Wes looked at Dan, doubt in his eyes. 'Wal, I guess I don't know fer shore.' He paused as if trying to recollect some fact which would pin-point the rustlers as Broken U riders. Suddenly the words poured from his lips. 'They couldn't be anyone else,' he yelled. 'Brooks sent word fer us to turn south. He was the only one who knew we were goin' thet way. Sent us right into a trap.' Wes glared at the rancher as he thought of his dead comrades.

'Jest steady up, son,' drawled Dan calmly. 'What you say could be right but it isn't likely.'

'Who else could it be?' snapped Wes angrily.

'Other folks did know about Brooks's message an' I got my suspicions about two of 'em but I can't prove anythin' yet, so jest calm down a bit an' maybe you'll give me somethin' to work on.'

Bridges glared at the faces around him and nodded at the sheriff.

'All right,' he said. He looked sharply at Brooks. 'I shore hope you're right, Sheriff, or I'll kill thet man fer what happened out there.' Bridges took a long drink before he continued. 'Wal, we turned south, trustin' Brooks's word. We pushed the herd fast 'cos the grazin' wasn't good and making the tour was throwin' us behind schedule. About twenty miles from the other ford, two days ago it would be, they hit us at dawn. Camp was hardly awake and they caught us napping. We never had a chance; wiped us out an' got the cattle as easy as that. Guess I must hev rolled under a wagon when I was hit and they must have missed me if they checked up see if everyone was dead.

'Did you see any of them?' asked Dan anxiously.

'Wal, it was barely light an' things happened so suddenly, but I did see some of 'em were masked.'

'What do you mean, some of 'em?' puzzled Dan. 'What about the others?'

'Wal, I figure they were Mex,' replied Bridges.

'Mex!' Dan was startled. He straightened quickly and looked sharply at Clint.

Astonishment crossed the old man's face. 'Gonzales!' he muttered.

Jack whistled with surprise. 'Thought he'd gone back over the border,' he said.

'Yeah, so he did,' replied Dan, 'but he showed up a year ago when some of the herders went south. We nearly got him then but he was jest one too many for us.' Dan paused and rubbed his chin thoughtfully. 'Funny how he's shown up both times cattle moved south. Wonder how he got to know?'

'Him,' snarled Bridges nodding towards Brooks.

'So could a number of other folks,' snapped Dan in reply. 'Forget thet until it's proved an' forget it quick because Brooks is goin' to take you to my house.' He turned to the rancher. 'Explain to Barbara an' then git

Bill Collins to take over here.' Dan grabbed his Stetson. 'Clint, Jack, Howard, c'm on, we ride after Gonzales!'

Chapter 11

Dan rode at a fast pace until they neared the Bar X buildings close to Wayman's Ford.

'What we slowin' fer?' queried Clint as the pace slackened.

'Don't want Pickering to see us in a hurry, he might figure we're on to somethin',' replied Dan.

The deputy looked at the sheriff with surprise. 'But Pickering couldn't hev had anythin' to do with this cattle stealin'.'

'Couldn't he?' muttered Dan. 'I've a hunch there may be more in this than coincidence. Keep your eyes open.' Cowboys eyed them curiously as they approached the buildings but all appeared normal to the four riders. As they slowed to a walk Matt Pickering's dark eyes watched them suspiciously from his cabin.

'What did you do with your horse, Curley?' snapped Pickering over his shoulder.

'Tied up in the barn,' replied the travel-stained cowboy surprised by the sharpness of the question. 'Anything wrong, boss?'

'Jest thet the nosey sheriff is prowlin' round again.' Pickering turned from the window. 'Git out the back an' stay with thet horse until I come fer you.'

'O.K., boss,' replied Curley jumping to his feet. 'He'd better not git too nosey,' he grinned patting his holster. He grabbed his battered Stetson and hurried out of the back door.

Pickering watched the riders for a moment longer before stepping out on to the veranda.

'Hi, there, Sheriff,' he called, leaning on the rail. 'Looking fer the usual?'

'Yeah,' answered Dan, but made no attempt to turn in Pickering's direction.

Matt laughed loud. 'You're wastin' your time. I've told you before, I don't know where those four hands are and Luke's ridden north.'

Dan nodded and rode on without a word.

Matt watched them with laughing eyes. Suddenly he started, amusement vanished. He narrowed his eyes staring at the horses.

'You've shore been in a mighty hurry,' Pickering muttered to himself. 'An' it hasn't been jest to look around here.' A puzzled frown furrowed his forehead as he pushed his Stetson back on his head.

He watched the horsemen ride to the river and slowly cross the ford. Hastily he unhitched his horse from the rail and swung quickly into the saddle.

'Curley!' he shouted as he reached the barn door. 'C'm on, we ride.'

Curley prompted by the urgency of the shout soon appeared, climbed into the saddle and turned his mount alongside his boss. They rode quickly towards the Brazo, but by the time they reached the river the sheriff and his three companions had disappeared round the bend in the trail. Pickering and his sidekick splashed through the water urging their horses forward, but once they were on the far bank they proceeded with great care. Cautiously they rounded the bend and kept the four riders in sight.

Dan held the same slow pace for a further mile. Pickering was beginning to think his hunch was wrong when the lawmen pushed their horses into a steady gallop. Matt increased his pace to keep them in sight but reined his horse to a halt when he saw them turn south at a fork in the trail.

'Guess thet brother Luke didn't do as he

was told,' muttered Matt angrily as he stared at the cloud of dust which marked the progress of the four riders.

Curley looked at him curiously. 'What you mean?' he asked.

'I reckon thet McCoy's headin' fer the herds trailin' south; figure he must have heard about the rustlin'.'

'But how could he?' gasped Curley.

'Don't know, unless Luke hasn't been certain there were no survivors.'

'What do we do now, boss?'

'You ride and warn Luke and Gonzales thet McCoy an' his sidekicks are about and may be on to somethin'. There's nothin' to connect us with Gonzales so maybe McCoy's jest investigating a rustling by a Mex. He's clever so be careful you aren't seen.'

'Couldn't we outride 'em an' bushwack 'em?' suggested Curley eagerly.

Pickering shook his head. 'Too risky,' he replied. 'It'd bring the law down in force and things would be too hot. All we want is to force the herds back into usin' Wayman's Ford an' then we can enforce legal toll again.'

Curley nodded. 'O.K., boss, I'll be careful.'

'Tell Luke I'll join him in a few days an'

you keep me informed how things are.'

Curley raised his hand in acknowledgment and kicked his horse forward. Matt watched him go, then turned his horse to retrace his steps to the Bar X.

Dan and his friends swung off the trail and rode at a hard pace, keeping to the ridge overlooking the trail which the herds would follow. The sheriff strained his eyes searching for the tell-tale cloud of dust which would disclose the presence of the Broken U second herd.

'Hope Gonzales hasn't jumped them yet,' muttered Dan.

'If Wes Bridges is right then he won't and never will,' said Jack.

Dan did not reply and they rode on in silence. After half an hour Dan suddenly called attention to a thin veil of dust which rose some distance ahead. They spurred their horses faster and were soon looking down on a huge herd of bellowing steers being forced onward by the flank riders and dragmen.

Dan reined his horse to a halt, pulled his spy glass from its buckskin scabbard and studied the herd carefully.

'Broken U,' he announced. 'They're makin' a good pace.' He turned to his deputy. 'You know this countryside, Clint, where do you reckon Gonzales might attack?'

Clint stroked his chin thoughtfully. 'Wal, I'm surprised to see the herd here. I figured Gonzales might hev hit it where he did his rustlin' a year ago.'

'There,' said Jack, 'he's let this one through, he must be workin' with Brooks.'

'Don't forgit he rustled the Crooked Z further south, about twenty miles from the ford,' pointed out Howard.

'Yeah,' agreed Clint, 'and I figure maybe he'll jump this one somewhere in the same area. Thet's in them maze of hills up ahead. Ideal fer cattle to disappear an' fer a gang to hide out – take some findin'.' He paused and scratched his head. 'Reckon they should reach there day after tomorrow.'

'Right,' said Dan. 'We'll work in pairs. Clint an' Jack keep tag on this herd. Howard and I will scout ahead fer signs of Gonzales.'

The three men nodded agreement and Dan and Howard shoved their horses to outride the herd and head for the distant hills. The day wore on without a sign of life once the herd was left behind. Suddenly Howard pulled his horse to a halt. He pointed to a small cloud of dust which moved swiftly below the skyline to their left.

'Some horseman in a mighty hurry over in thet hollow,' observed Howard.

Dan kicked his horse forward. 'C'm on,' he shouted. 'Worth investagatin'.' He turned his black towards the hollow to reach the edge ahead of the unknown rider. As they neared the edge he took out his spy glass, slipped from the saddle and doubling up ran quickly forward. He flung himself down on his stomach to gaze into the hollow. Howard was beside him and silently they watched the cowboy approach.

Howard narrowed his eyes. 'Looks as if he's been doin' some hard ridin'.'

Dan raised his spy-glass to his eye and watched for a moment before speaking. 'Seen this hombre in town,' he muttered. 'Know him, Howard?' He passed the spy-glass to his companion.

Howard focused on the rider and studied him carefully. Suddenly he gasped. 'Bar X.'

'We're on to it, Howard,' cried Dan. 'You're shore?'

'I've seen him with the Bar X cowpokes once or twice if thet's sufficient to go on,' replied Howard.

'It's sufficient fer me,' answered Dan. 'C'm on.' He turned and crawled Indian fashion away from the hollow and then rising to his feet ran swiftly to the horses. Howard followed suit and soon they were in the saddles shadowing the unsuspecting rider.

The cowboy did not falter but kept his horse at a fast but steady pace. He swung out of the hollow, crossed the ridge and dropped down the gentle slope to the trail which he followed to the distant hills. Dan and Howard followed silently, keeping the rider just in sight and carefully using what cover they could. As they neared the hills Dan quickened the pace to close the gap, realising that he must take some risk of being seen otherwise they would lose the lone cowboy in the hills.

When they reached the higher ground the man from the Bar X left the trail and entered a valley which ran into the hill country. Dan and Howard followed cautiously as the valley narrowed. They lost sight of the cowboy as he turned the bend ahead. Dan slowed when they reached the corner and rode carefully round. Suddenly he pulled his mount to a halt and cursed under his breath. He motioned with his hand for Howard to keep quiet.

'Can't hear his horse,' he whispered. 'I don't like it but I–'

His words were rudely interrupted by the crash of a rifle and the whine of a bullet as it sang over their heads. They flung themselves from their horses which, frightened by the noise, spun round flaying the air with their forefeet. Dan and Howard dived for cover.

'He's rumbled us,' muttered Howard as they lay in the dust behind some rocks.

Dan cursed, pulled his Colt from its holster and reached for his sombrero which had fallen from his head as he plunged to the ground.

'It's an old trick,' he muttered, 'but we'll see.'

He placed the dusty sombrero on the barrel of his Colt and slowly poked it round the side of the rock. The rifle crack reverberated round the valley as the sombrero was sent spinning in the dust.

'Good marksman,' whispered Howard. 'He knows what he's about.'

'I figure he means to keep us here until dark an' then slip away,' said Dan looking round desperately for some means of outwitting this cowboy. 'We've got to make him move soon,' he said anxiously.

'Yeah, but what can we do?' puzzled Howard.

'I'm going to make a dash fer thet big boulder over there.' Dan nodded to a huge rock about thirty yards away.

'You can't, he'll drop you easy,' protested Howard.

'I'll make it,' said Dan. 'You poke your gun out to attract his attention an' I'll make a dash for it. I'll be there before he can get a bead on me especially if you blaze away to keep him down.'

Howard nodded. 'What then?'

'You keep his attention and I'll work up above him. There's plenty of cover once I git to thet boulder.'

'Right,' agreed Howard. 'I'm ready.'

'O.K. Now,' shouted Dan and waited a split second for Howard to show his gun.

The crash had hardly split the silence when Dan leaped to his feet and, bending forward, raced towards the boulder. The valley filled with the sound of guns as Howard blazed away in the direction of the hidden marksman. Dust spurted in front of Dan. A second shot whistled past his head and in desperation Dan flung himself forward as a third bullet ricocheted off the boulder in front of him. Dan hit the ground behind the rock, driving all the breath from his body. For a few moments he lay panting, gulping air into his heaving lungs. Once he had recovered his breath he turned to plan his way up the hillside. Bullets whined over the boulder and Dan waited patiently until Howard returned the fire to divert the unwelcome attention which the Bar X man was giving to him.

Dan meticulously picked his way forward, setting his feet and hands down with the utmost care so as not to send any loose stones rolling to betray his presence. Inch by inch he moved carefully upwards. He quickened his pace and immediately cursed his carelessness as a shower of stones rolled down the slope. A rapid volley of shots flew in Dan's direction. Suddenly they stopped. Suspicion filled Dan's mind and cautiously he peered over the rock which sheltered him.

The cowboy, realising he was being out-manoeuvred, was swinging on to his horse, turning it along the valley as he did so. Dan leaped to his feet, pulling his Colt from its holster.

'The horses, Howard, the horses!' he yelled.

Howard had seen Dan jump from cover and was already on his feet. He raced down the valley to the horses which had galloped away when the firing started and now champed grass a quarter of a mile away.

The cowboy had flattened himself along his horse's back and put it into a full gallop. The animal stretched itself and in answer to its rider's bidding weaved along the valley as Dan emptied his Colt after them.

As his gun clicked on the empty chamber Dan raced down the hillside to meet Howard. Howard hauled on the reins but Dan was in the saddle before the horses stopped. They shoved their horses forward and raced along the valley in pursuit of the lone rider who had wasted no time in widening the gap between himself and the lawmen.

Chapter 12

Curley grinned as he flattened himself along his horse's back and weaved along the valley at a fast gallop. Bullets whistled harmlessly around and soon he was out of range. He had a good lead on his pursuers and was confident that with his knowledge of the hills he could soon lose them.

He kept his horse at a hard pace as he turned from one valley to another and crossed a number of low ridges. The lowering sun was casting long shadows as he turned into a smaller valley which ran to the south-west. He rode steadily onwards and darkness blanketed the countryside by the time he reached a fork in the valley. He pulled his panting horse to a stop and for a few moments sat still, his head inclined to the way he had come. No sound broke the silence.

A wide stream flowed from the right hand fork; Curley crossed it quickly and rode on to the hillside. Once more he listened carefully but all was quiet. He pushed his horse forward, climbing steadily until he reached a rougher stony surface. After a further twenty yards he turned at right angles and rode along the hillside for a quarter of a mile. He then turned down towards the stream but on reaching the edge of the rough ground which had hidden his tracks he dismounted and led his horse carefully downhill, making sure to obliterate all traces of this fresh trail. He took his horse into the water and made certain that he had left no sign of his presence on the bank before he straightened with a deep sigh of satisfaction.

Curley chuckled to himself as he climbed into the saddle. 'Thet'll keep you guessing, Mister Sheriff,' he muttered as he shoved his horse forward in the water.

The animal was not happy as the water swirled around its fetlocks, but its rider encouraged it and steadily they moved upstream.

The tiny valley narrowed, the sides becoming cliff-like, stark and black, darkening the night around the lone rider. After half a mile a huge wall of rock rose in front and the valley turned sharply to the left. Curley slipped from the animal's back and led it through the swift flowing stream. He breathed a sigh of relief as he rounded the turn, for now the distant crash of falling water reached his ears. He hurried onward.

The narrow valley became little more than a cut, the sides towering to the star-studded canopy of night. Suddenly the walls of rock turned to meet, and from the overhanging rock a waterfall plunged a hundred and fifty feet in a single drop to bounce in spray off the rock bed and run away in the stream which hid Curley's tracks.

The lone cowboy halted before a veil of water half hidden in the darkness. He raised his head towards the top of the rock face sharply marked against the night sky. He cupped his hands round his mouth and the bark of a coyote rose above the pounding water. Five seconds passed and the bark sounded again to be answered by three similar barks.

Curley patted his horse's neck. 'You'll soon be under cover,' he comforted.

He pulled the animal forward towards the waterfall, then moved to one side round the main drop to come on to a flat rock which formed the floor of a huge hollow running back into the cliff. The cowboy led his mount into the darkness carefully feeling his way along the wall of rock until he reached a split in the rock face. Curley looked up to see the canopy of night bridging a narrow crack which ran to the left.

He edged forward, his feet slipping on the rocks worn smooth by frequent use. The horse hesitated but Curley spoke softly to the animal as he urged it through the cleft. The dark walls gave way to a lighter hue as the end of the passage came in sight.

Suddenly a voice rapped, echoing along the cleft. 'Who's there?'

'Bar X.' Curley gave the password quickly, knowing that the Mexican guard would soon send a bullet in his direction if he hesitated.

'All right,' replied the unseen Mexican.

Curley moved swiftly to the end of the cleft. High precipitous hills enclosed a narrow valley and lights gleamed from a group of buildings a quarter of a mile away. The cowboy swung into the saddle and without a further word to the guard kicked his horse forward.

At the sound of the hard-ridden horse men from Bar X and Mexicans flung open doors to pierce the night with two shafts of light. Curley hauled his horse to a sliding halt in front of the first door.

'Curley!' gasped Luke Pickering as the light revealed the unexpected rider. 'What are you doing back to soon?'

The weary man swung from the saddle.

'Trouble,' he said curtly.

The Mexicans and the Bar X men crowded round at this news but their murmurings were cut short by the tall slim man who stood next to Luke.

'Quiet, you good-for-nothing crew! There's no trouble that I, Gonzales, can't handle. Go back to your bunks and dream of your nice fat senoritas. Mister Curley, you come inside.' He swung on his heel and walked into the ranch-house.

Curley turned to the crowd. 'Here, Shorty, look after my hoss,' he said, tossing the reins to a small thick-set man. 'And, Cookie, rustle me some grub, it's a long time since I ate.'

He stepped on to the veranda where Luke stood waiting.

'Is Matt all right?' asked Luke anxiously.

Curley nodded and the two Bar X men entered the ranch-house. Gonzales lighted a long, pencil-thin cigar from the fire and swung round to face them as Luke closed the door. He took a long draw at the tobacco and blew the smoke into the air.

'Well, Curly, what ees this trouble?' he asked.

Luke nodded towards the whisky bottle which stood on the table and after charging a glass Curley related the reason for his quick return and told of his brush with the sheriff and Howard Collins.

'You did well to outsmart this Dan McCoy, from what I hear he ees a smart hombre,' said Gonzales stroking his moustache.

'But why didn't you kill him?' snapped Luke.

'Matt said not to on account of bringing the law down in force,' explained Curley.

'Matt's too soft,' snarled Luke pacing the floor.

'But very wise,' remarked Gonzales softly.

'Wise?' mocked Luke. 'You're as soft as my brother. What's wise in leavin' a man alive who can wreck our set-up?'

Gonzales narrowed his dark eyes. 'Luke, you're a hot-head. You'll have us in trouble unless you think first.'

'Think! There's no time for niceties in this game. You should know thet, Gonzales,' stormed Luke. Contempt showed in his face as he paced the floor. He slapped his holster. 'That's where power is,' he shouted, his eyes blazing. 'The law of the gun has no answer. That's how we can win.'

'Enough, Luke!' The order cracked like a whip and Luke froze in his tracks. Slowly he turned to face a Gonzales whose stern face halted the retort which sprang to his lips. 'I'm in command here and when you operate at this end you will obey me.'

Luke Pickering stared blackly at the Mexican whose dark eyes pierced him. Slowly he relaxed and as the tension eased the Mexican's voice softened.

'That ees better, Mister Luke. Your brother would be pleased to see you agree with me.' He paused, stroking his moustache thoughtfully. 'I think it better if we take this herd at the south end of the pass instead of the north. No doubt the sheriff will know where we struck last time, maybe this will fox him.'

'But that's goin' to make a longer drive back here,' objected Luke.

The tall Mexican smiled. 'I'll drive them straight to the border,' he said, 'an' no one will follow us if you do your job properly an' see that there are *no* survivors this time.'

Luke stirred uneasily.

'In the meantime,' continued Gonzales, 'we will post a reception committee in case Mister Sheriff ees lucky enough to stumble on our hide-out.'

As darkness closed across the hills Dan and Howard found it more difficult to follow Curley's trail. Eventually Dan pulled his horse to a halt.

'It's no use, Howard,' he sighed. 'We'll hev to give up fer the night.'

Howard nodded his agreement. 'This is as good a place as any to bed down,' he commented, and the two lawmen were soon between their blankets.

Dan stirred as the sun flooded the Texas countryside with the first light of day. He found Howard already up with breakfast sizzling in the pan. The hot coffee drove warmth into his body.

As soon as breakfast was over they kicked out the fire, packed their belongings, and climbed into the saddle.

They soon picked up Curley's trail and were able to maintain a rapid progress until Dan's experienced eyes noted Curley's halt at the fork. Dan swung from the saddle and examined the ground thoroughly.

'Wonder why he halted here an' then turned to the stream?' puzzled Dan.

'It looks as if he didn't know which way he wanted to go,' replied Howard.

'Yeah,' said Dan, 'but thet's strange; I reckon the way he twisted through these hills he knew where he was goin' all right. C'm on, all we can do is to follow.' Dan climbed into the saddle and pushed his horse forward to the stream.

The trail was clearly visible on the other side and they followed it steadily up the hill until they reached the stony ground where the tracks disappeared.

'Do you think he went over the top?' asked Howard, indicating the height above.

Dan rubbed his chin. 'I wonder,' he muttered. 'Seems to me thet we were meant to lose the trail up here. Maybe he went back down again.' The sheriff swung his horse round. 'C'm on,' he called.

Dan sent the black slithering and sliding down the hillside, splashed across the stream and pulled up at the spot where Curley had halted. He looked at Howard who pulled his horse to a halt beside Dan.

'I reckon his trail to here is genuine; thet other's a blind.'

'Then you figure he used one of these valleys?' said Frank.

Dan nodded. 'But which one?' he mused. After a moment he indicated the valley to the left. 'Let's try this one.'

They worked slowly searching for some sign which would betray Curley's movements. After two miles of fruitless search Dan called to Howard.

'Seems we're in the wrong valley. Let's git back an' try the other.' They galloped back to the fork and followed the stream along the other valley. After ten minutes' search Dan slipped from the saddle.

'He's vanished completely,' said Howard as he stopped alongside the sheriff. Dan frowned and pushed back his Stetson.

'We can't be right,' continued Howard. 'There isn't a sign at all; besides, look at that wall of rock; it swings round and seals off this valley; we're riding to a dead-end.'

'Maybe,' replied Dan, 'but these hills can be deceiving. Let's eat and decide what to do.'

Howard swung from the saddle and the two men soon had a meal ready. The horses wandered to the stream for a drink and Dan watched them, his mind occupied with the thought of the vanished Curley. Suddenly he jumped to his feet.

'Fools!' he yelled. 'Those horses hev more sense.'

Howard looked at the sheriff in amazement. 'What's bitten you?' he asked.

Dan spun on his heels to face Howard. 'The horses hev found the answer,' he shouted excitedly. 'Curley rode in the stream!'

'No wonder we didn't find any tracks,' said Howard eagerly. 'Why didn't we think of it before?'

The meal was finished quickly and they climbed into the saddles to follow the stream with a renewed enthusiasm.

The walls of the valley crowded in upon them, dark, frowning, overpowering even in daylight. As they neared the rock face they saw that the valley turned. They grinned at each other, spirits high, feeling that at least they were on the right track.

'Waterfall ahead,' observed Howard as the pound of falling water reached their ears.

Their hopes dropped when they saw the narrow valley close in front of them and their way barred by the veil of water falling in front of the rock face. They pulled their horses to a halt and a puzzled frown creased Dan's forehead as he looked around him.

'This place gives me the creeps, Dan.' Howard found himself speaking in a whisper.

'Not so much the creeps but a feeling of being watched,' answered Dan quietly. He swung from his horse and walked slowly forward towards the fall. The spray flew around him before he stopped. Shielding his eyes he peered at the falling water.

'What you figurin'?' asked Howard as he joined Dan.

'This water falls free from the face of the rock an' I wondered what it was like behind it,' answered Dan.

'We could git round thet side,' suggested Howard pointing to the right.

He was about to step forward when a rifle crashed above the noise of the water. A bullet spanged the ground at their feet and both men jumped back in surprise. They looked up to see a figure, with rifle pointing downwards, standing on the top of the cliff.

'A Mex!' gasped Dan. 'We've found it, Howard!'

'You've found it all right,' said a voice behind them.

They spun round to find themselves staring into the muzzles of rifles held by four Mexicans. A fifth, taller and slimmer stood in front of them.

'You're a little too curious, Mister Mc-Coy.' The tall man spoke softly, a faint smile playing on his lips.

Dan stared at the handsome Mexican who stood feet astride full of self-assurance. A tall sugar-loafed, grey sombrero crowned his head. Its long chin strap of braided rawhide hung to a knot on his blue silk shirt which was covered by a short patterned vest. A wide sash topped tight dark trousers.

'Gonzales!' muttered Dan.

The Mexican's eyes flashed a smile as he bowed.

'At your service, Sheriff. We've been expecting you. Your progress has been watched along this valley. Had you turned and gone back we should not have detained you, but your curiosity to see what is behind that falling veil must be satisfied.'

He turned to one of the four Mexicans and

spoke quickly to him. The Mexican stepped forward and disarmed the two lawmen.

'And now, my friends,' continued Gonzales with a smile, 'the secret will be revealed to you. Follow me.' He stepped forward only to stop suddenly. A serious expression replaced the laughter in his dark eyes. 'I must warn you not to try any tricks; my men are rather nervous on the trigger.'

Rifles prodded the Texans forward and they kept close on the Mexican's heels as he moved round the fall and into the dark hollow behind. They worked their way through the narrow cleft until they came out into the valley.

'There, my friends, is the place you have been looking for.' Gonzales swept his arms in the direction of the wooden buildings along the valley. 'The hideout of Pancho Gonzales when he operates in Texas,' he announced proudly.

A group of horses were held by a dark swarthy Mexican and as soon as the lawmen's mounts had been brought through the cleft they climbed into the saddles and galloped to the ranch-house.

Six cowboys leaned on the rail watching their approach. Dan narrowed his eyes. His suspicions were confirmed; the Pickerings worked with Gonzales!

'Wal, wal, if it ain't McCoy,' mocked Luke Pickering. He turned to the men beside him. 'Curley, you'll remember him from yesterday. Shorty, Zeke, Walt, Buck, you'll remember thet you were the sheriff's guests a short while ago.' He grinned as he faced Dan. 'They're all sorry they couldn't stay with you any longer but I guess you'll understand.'

They roared with laugher. Gonzales rapped an order to two of his gang who stepped forward, hauled the Texans roughly from the saddles and pushed them up the steps of the ranch-house. They were escorted unceremoniously to a room at the back of the house and thrust inside. Before they could get to their feet the door slammed and the lock was turned.

Chapter 13

Matt Pickering was uneasy as he rode back to the Bar X after leaving Curley. McCoy was a man who needed watching. Why had he ridden south with three sidekicks? Pickering frowned. He must have heard about the rustling but how much did he know? Pickering tried to occupy himself when he got back to the Bar X, but his thoughts kept turning to the hills to the south. He tried to reassure himself that all would be well with Gonzales in command, but he knew what a hot-head his brother could be. He wished he had gone south too, but the sheriff would have been suspicious if the Bar X had been deserted.

Matt had a sleepless night and the next morning after breakfast he could contain himself no longer. He must try to find out where the sheriff had gone and what was known in town. He saddled his horse and rode quickly to Red Springs.

The town was quiet and Matt rode slowly along Main Street to pull up outside the Silver Dollar. He swung out of the saddle and hitched his horse to the rail. Nodding to three men who lounged on the sidewalk, he pushed open the batwings and strode into the saloon.

'Usual, George,' he said curtly as he leaned on the bar and pushed his sombrero to the back of his head.

The bartender placed a bottle in front of Matt who poured himself a drink.

'You missed the excitement yesterday,

Mister Pickering,' said George wiping the counter with his cloth.

'Excitement?' asked Pickering trying to appear casual.

'Haven't you heard?' retorted the surprised barman. 'Some cowpoke rode in here badly shot up. Shortly afterwards the sheriff rode out of town with Clint Schofield and the Collins boys – and they didn't waste time putting the town behind them.'

'Who was this hombre?' asked Matt.

'They call him Wes Bridges and they say he's the only survivor from one of the herds trailing south.'

'Only survivor? What do you mean?'

'Wal, no one seems to know exactly what happened but they say the sheriff's ridden after Gonzales.'

'Gonzales!' Matt appeared surprised.

'Yeah. Seems he may be back in operation in the hills.' The barman moved away when another cowboy called for a drink.

Matt stared moodily at his glass. So the sheriff knew about Gonzales but it appeared that he had not connected the Pickerings with the Mexican. However, Matt felt uneasy. He knew how persistent Dan could be. He felt that he needed a trump card in case the sheriff found out the truth.

Suddenly he finished his drink in one gulp, threw a coin on the counter and hurried from the saloon. He unhitched his horse, climbed into the saddle and rode slowly along Main Street past the false-fronted shops, the Wells Fargo office and the livery stable to the trim wooden houses flanked by neat gardens on the edge of town. He slipped from the saddle in front of one with white painted railings and hurried along the path. His tap on the door was answered by Barbara McCoy, who although amazed to see Matt Pickering, hid her surprise.

'Ma'm,' said Pickering respectfully removing his sombrero, 'I'm afraid I have some bad news for you.'

Alarm crossed Barbara's face, her eyes widening, voicing the unspoken question, 'What's happened to Dan?'

'Your husband's been brought to the Bar X after a bad fall.' Pickering saw Barbara's alarm and quickly reassured her. 'He'll be all right but he's askin' fer you.'

Relief showed on her face. 'Come inside, Mister Pickering,' she said stepping aside. 'I'll change into something more suitable for riding. It's a pity you weren't here a few minutes sooner, the doctor's just left.'

Matt was startled by this information but

he gathered his thoughts quickly. 'Oh! I've sent one of my men for him so you needn't worry. I hope the doctor wasn't payin' a professional visit.'

'Well, he was.' Barbara laughed when she saw the concern on Pickering's face. 'Oh, but he didn't come to see me. Haven't you heard about the attack on the Crooked Z herd?'

'I heard rumours in town. They say that some badly shot cowboy brought the news.'

'Yes, that's right and that's why the doctor called; I'm looking after him.'

Pickering was taken aback by this news but outwardly he kept calm.

Barbara turned to go upstairs. 'I won't be a moment. Would you mind saddling my horse, it would save time?'

'Certainly,' said Matt and left the house. He hurried to the stable cursing his luck. No one connected him with the rustling but now this cowpoke would know that Mrs McCoy was leaving with him and suspicion would be roused when the alarm was raised and if he left without her Barbara would be suspicious. His thoughts raced as he threw the saddle on to the horse. If luck was with him it might be possible to eliminate the cowpoke before he told anyone where

Barbara had gone.

With the horse ready Matt grew impatient as the minutes ticked by but smiled when Barbara appeared, neatly dressed in a yellow silk blouse with a red scarf tied at her throat. Her jeans were neatly folded in to the top of high-heeled, brightly polished boots and a white sombrero hung from the braided cord around her neck. She swung gracefully into the saddle, and with Pickering alongside her, headed away from the town at a fast gallop.

They soon reached the Bar X, and as they pulled up outside the ranch-house Pickering yelled for one of his men.

'Git all the boys saddled up, we ride, an' send Blackie to me,' rasped Pickering.

'Right, boss,' answered the cowboy, and hurried away calling to the rest of the outfit.

A puzzled expression clouded Barbara's face. 'You aren't leaving Dan here, are you?'

'No,' smiled Matt, 'because he isn't here!'

Barbara gasped. 'Not here? But you said–'

'Never mind what I said,' retorted Pickering. 'We're riding and you're comin' with us.'

Anger flared in Barbara's eyes. 'I'm not. Is this some kind of joke? Where's Dan?'

'I haven't seen him since he crossed Wayman's Ford yesterday,' smirked Pickering.

'What!' Barbara straightened herself in the saddle, her eyes flashing annoyance at the rancher.

'Your husband's too nosey and if he gits too near the truth about my game then you could be a mighty nice asset to me, Mrs McCoy.'

Barbara gasped. The colour drained from her face. 'Kidnapped!'

Pickering smirked.

Barbara's eyes flamed. She was annoyed that she had fallen for the trick. Impulsively she pulled her horse round but Pickering, quick to see her attempt to break away, pulled his horse sharply towards Barbara and crowded her against the veranda rail.

Pickering's eyes narrowed. 'I wouldn't try to escape. I aim to treat you gently, but I have some rough cowpokes if the need arises,' he warned coldly.

A dark swarthy man with black beard galloped up. 'You want me, boss?' he rasped hoarsely.

Barbara glanced at the newcomer and recoiled as his eyes met hers. She quickly diverted her look from the cold, dark evil eyes which peered from two deep hollows.

'Yeah, Blackie,' answered Pickering.

'There's a wounded cowpoke at McCoy's. I guess he'll know that Mrs McCoy left with me. I don't want to be connected with her disappearance so he'll hev to be eliminated.'

Blackie grinned and without a word swung his horse round and sent the animal galloping towards Red Springs.

Barbara's breath came quickly. 'You fiend,' she shouted, striking at Pickering.

Matt laughed at the weak blows and caught her wrists. She twisted and fought until with a hard jerk Pickering tumbled her from the saddle. She fell solidly to the ground and lay gasping for breath. Pickering sat unmoved on his horse. Slowly she raised her head, tears in her eyes.

'Let's hev no more nonsense, Mrs McCoy, next time I'll take more drastic measures. Now, git on thet horse, we ride.'

Barbara looked round hopefully but all she saw was the Bar X cowhands riding towards them ready for the trail.

Blackie slowed his galloping horse to a steady trot as he neared Red Springs. Not wishing to attract attention, he rode steadily along Main Street. Suddenly he started – a horse was tied to the railings outside the sheriff's house! He slipped from the saddle quickly and, seeing no one about, hurried along the path. He pushed the front door open gently and stepped swiftly inside. He paused momentarily, listening for any sound. Footsteps crossed the landing above and he heard a door open.

'Hello, Wes,' someone greeted.

'Hello, Mister Collins,' came the reply.

The door muffled the next remark as it swung shut. Blackie realised he must act quickly before Mrs McCoy's father was told where she was.

Quietly he mounted the stairs two at a time, drawing his Colt as he did so. The voices became clearer when he reached the landing.

'Too bad about the sheriff, wasn't it?' said Wes.

'Dan? What's happened?' alarm showed in Bill Collins' voice.

Blackie was beside the door, thankful that it had not been closed on its catch. Gently he pushed it slightly open and to his relief saw that the bed was directly opposite the door. Slowly he raised his Colt.

'Hadn't you heard? He had an accident and Mrs McCoy—'

The words were lost in the crash of the Colt. Bill Collins spun round, his gun leaping to his hand, but already the door had slammed shut. He heard footsteps race across the landing and they were already half way down the stairs when he flung open the door only to twist back as lead splinted the doorpost.

He scrambled to his feet as the front door closed with a crash. Collins tore down the stairs, hurled the front door open to see a cowboy galloping down the street. He raised his gun, pumping lead in the direction of the flying hoofs. Suddenly the horse reared and with a scream of pain spun round and crashed to the ground, sending its rider spinning in the dust.

Collins ran towards him, but he was sent diving for cover when the cowboy raised himself and fired. The killer leaped to his feet, doubled up and ran for the sidewalk, flinging himself flat as Collins emptied one Colt. Men who had hurried on to the street at the first sound of gunfire took cover as the lead flew. Blackie looked round for some means of escape. An alleyway lay twenty-five yards from him and fear left his eyes when he saw it. He sent a hail of lead towards Collins, crept swiftly to the wall of the building and started to inch his way along, using all the available cover.

Realising Blackie's intention, Collins moved swiftly forward only to be sent diving again by Blackie's bullets. Blackie seized this moment to make his dash. He leaped to his feet, but as he did so a man slipped from a shop doorway. Blackie, intent on reaching the alley, saw him too late. He raised his arm to fire but death reached him first from the smoking gun of the man on the sidewalk. Blackie crashed to the boards and lay still.

Bill Collins ran forward. 'Thanks, Brooks,' he panted.

Brooks shoved his gun back into its holster. 'Guessed thet hombre was up to no good, if you wanted him.'

'He's jest killed Wes Bridges!' announced Collins.

'What!' gasped Brooks.

Collins turned to the cowboys who had clustered round. 'Two of you tidy up here; the rest saddle up, we need a posse.'

The group broke up and cowboys ran for their horses.

'This fella's one of Pickering's riders,' said Collins to Brooks, who looked puzzled by Bill's orders. 'I figure he was sent to stop Wes talkin'.'

'About what?' queried Brooks. 'He's told us all about the rustlin'.'

'Not sure,' answered Collins. 'Wes was tellin' me thet somethin' hed happened to Dan when this hombre killed him. Barbara's not at home. There could be a connection. Maybe Wes knew what it was and had to be stopped from talkin'.' Bill rubbed his chin. 'C'm on, we'll see what Pickering has to say.'

Twelve men pounded the road in urgent gallop towards the Bar X. Collins feared the worst for his daughter. He felt sure that Pickering was at the bottom of her disappearance. His eyes narrowed when he saw the Bar X spread. The posse pulled their horses to a dust-raising stop in front of the ranch-house. No one had moved to meet them and Bill Collins looked puzzled as he swung out of the saddle. Fear gripped his stomach at what he might find as he flung open the ranch-house door, but the room was empty.

'No one here,' he shouted. 'Some of you check the other buildings.'

Cowboys turned their horses but were soon back to report that the place was deserted.

'What do we do now?' asked Brooks.

Collins leaned on the rail. A worried frown creased his brow as he stared at the ground.

He shook his head slowly. 'I don't know,' he said wearily. His lips tightened. 'But if anything's happened to Babs or Dan I'll kill Pickering with my own hands.'

'Look here, Collins,' said Brooks. 'Dan set off after Gonzales. If Pickering and Gonzales are in this together then we may find our answer where the herds are trailin' to the southern ford.'

Collins looked up sharply. 'Maybe you're right,' he said eagerly. 'It's worth a try. C'm on, let's ride!'

Chapter 14

Bill Collins, his face drawn in grim lines, pushed the horses hard. Beside him, Brooks was also lost in his thoughts as the posse thundered onwards. With no trail to follow Collins knew it was a long shot they were playing. He kept the posse to the ridge above the valley, straining his eyes searching for the cloud of dust which would tell him that the Broken U herd had not suffered the same fate as the Crooked Z. It was late in the afternoon when he eased himself in the saddle with a grunt and pointed to a cloud of dust which rose above the horizon.

'Seems thet your outfit's all right,' he yelled to Brooks.

'Yeah,' answered the rancher with undisguised relief.

They rapidly overhauled the herd and were about to swing down the hillside when a rider appeared galloping towards them.

'Thet's Jack,' observed Collins as he turned to meet his son. 'Know the way he sits a horse.'

'What brings you out here, pa?' yelled Jack as he pulled his horse to a sliding halt in front of the posse. 'An' why a posse?' he added nodding to the riders who milled around.

'Pickering's taken Babs,' announced Collins, his face darkening.

'What!' gasped Jack. A puzzled look crossed his face. 'But why? What happened?'

Bill Collins quickly related what he knew. 'We've no definite proof thet it was Pickering,' he concluded, 'but I figure thet if we find him we'll find Barbara.'

Jack nodded grimly. 'Clint and I have been on this ridge all day and I can tell you thet no riders hev passed this way.'

His father sighed wearily. 'So Brooks's hunch thet he'd head this way was wrong.'

He shrugged his shoulders. 'Where's Dan? We'll hev to let him know.'

'Dan an' Howard went scouting in the hills and left Clint and I to shadow the herd. We've not heard from them since. I figure they should be ridin' in any time. Thet herd will camp at this end of the pass tonight and be in a likely place fer rustlin'. Guess you'd all better stick with us tonight.'

'An' what about Babs?' asked Bill Collins anxiously.

'Wherever Pickering's taken her I reckon he won't hev harmed her. I figure he's got scared and thinks she would be useful if things get too hot fer him. Hang on here, pa, until Dan gits back.'

Collins shrugged his shoulders resignedly and called to the posse to follow. They rode slowly along the hill top and soon joined Clint who, when he heard Bill's story, swore revenge on Pickering. After choosing a suitable site to camp, the cowboys watched the Broken U riders circle the herd to a halt and settle the steers for the night. Clint anxiously scanned the hills for some sign of Dan, but nothing moved in the dark expanse as night closed over the Texas countryside.

Barbara's anxious glances behind her were

not lost on Pickering.

'We aren't being followed,' he called, and laughed harshly.

Barbara ignored his remark and eased herself in the saddle. Suddenly alarmed, fear gripped her. She realised that they were riding west and that the hills which were mere folds on the horizon to the south were getting no nearer. Where was Pickering taking her? What had happened to Dan? The questions flashed across her mind to the beat of pounding hoofs.

Apart from brief halts Pickering rode at a fast pace until late in the afternoon he pulled in beneath the shade of some cottonwoods. Exhausted by the hard ride, Barbara half slipped and half fell from the saddle and sank wearily beneath a tree. Two cowboys built a rough shelter for Barbara whilst the rest prepared for the night's halt. She was too tired to notice the activity and she was almost asleep when she was aware of a man standing over her. She looked up to see Pickering holding out a plate of bacon and beans.

'You'll feel better with this inside you,' he said. 'You'll find a bed's been fixed fer you over there.' Pickering nodded towards a clump of trees. 'And don't git any wild ideas of trying to escape – there'll be guards on all night.'

Barbara took the plate without a word. As soon as she had finished the meal she climbed wearily to her feet, and as she walked towards the rough shelter she felt the eyes of all the men upon her. A shudder ran through her body and in spite of her tiredness sleep did not come easily as her mind filled with the evil faces of this rough bunch of riders. Now she knew that Dan's suspicions about Pickering were well founded. If only she could escape and contact him, but she realised that Pickering was no man to let her slip through his grasp now. Her eyes closed.

Suddenly she was startled by the ear-splitting roar of a Colt close at hand. She scrambled to her feet and pushed some branches aside. The night was dark but she recognised Pickering, back towards her shelter, standing over a still figure. Cowboys ran towards him.

'Don't let anyone else try thet,' he snarled. 'Mrs McCoy is being held in case her husband gits too nosey, and fer no other reason. Now, two of you git this hombre out of here.' Pickering pushed the Colt back in his holster, turning away from the grin scene and lay down close to the shelter.

Two hands stooped to pick up the dead man as the others shuffled back to their blankets. Barbara shuddered, tears filling her eyes. She flung herself on the ground and cried herself to sleep.

Dan and Howard quickly realised that the possibilities of escape from Gonzales' hideout were very slim.

'No use forcing the door,' observed Howard, 'we'd be cut down before we could git out.'

'Same at the window,' commented Dan. 'Gonzales has two guards watchin' it.'

Howard cursed and flung himself on the bed. 'You were right about Pickering and Gonzales. Wonder when they'll jump thet herd?'

Dan sat on the edge of the bed. 'Wish I knew,' he muttered.

The light was beginning to fade in the sky when a key turning in the lock brought the prisoners to their feet. The door swung back to reveal a smiling Gonzales.

'I want to talk to you, Meester Sheriff, come out here,' he said, and turned away from the door.

Dan looked sharply at Howard and knew he was ready should the slightest chance of escape present itself. As they went out into the room their hearts sank for two men with Colts drawn stood near the door.

Gonzales smiled as he turned to face them. He came straight to the point. 'Luke, here, wants to get rid of you now, but I don't go for this cold-blooded murder. I may be a cattle thief but at least I fight clean.'

'You're soft,' spat Luke, who lolled in a chair, his face black with hate.

The smile vanished from Gonzales' face and he spun round to face Luke. 'I'm boss here and what I say goes,' he snarled. He paused to let the words sink in before turning back to Dan and Howard. His voice was cold when he spoke again. 'I want some information – were there any other riders with you?'

'Thet's something we're keeping to ourselves,' answered Dan casually.

Luke jumped from the chair, his eyes blazing wildly.

'Oh, no it's not!' he yelled. 'I'll beat it out of you.'

Luke aimed a savage blow at Dan who, although he swayed backwards and took some of the weight from the punch, was sent sprawling across the floor. Howard stepped forward only to be halted by the menacing Colts of Luke's sidekicks. Luke, murder in his eyes, moved towards Dan. Gonzales jumped forward between them.

'That will do, Luke,' he snapped angrily. 'That won't do any good with McCoy nor Collins if I know my men.'

Luke glared at the Mexican, his eyes wild with fury. Hot retorts sprang to his lips only to be stifled as the cold, piercing eyes of Gonzales bore into him. Like a whipped dog he turned away. As Dan struggled to his feet he made a lunge at Gonzales' holster but the Mexican noticing the movement, stepped sideways and chopped Dan to the floor with a hard blow to the back of the neck.

'I too can play rough if necessary, Meester Sheriff,' he snapped between closed teeth. He looked at Howard. 'Take him back in there,' he ordered, nodding to the back room.

Dan's head spun as Howard helped him to the bed and the door slammed behind them.

Sleep came hard to the two lawmen. Their hopes that some opportunity for escape would present itself were not fulfilled. The guards outside the window were too vigilant and they knew it was useless to attempt to break through the door. Their uneasy night came to an end with arrival of breakfast.

Mid-way through the morning Dan

sprang to his feet and moved swiftly to the window. A moment passed before he spoke.

'Come here, Howard,' he whispered urgently. 'Do you hear horses?'

Howard hurried to the window and listened carefully.

'Yes,' he nodded. 'And there's a lot of 'em.'

A chair scraped in the next room.

'They've heard 'em,' said Dan who, together with Howard, moved over to the door to listen.

They heard the riders arrive amidst much shouting, but although they strained their ears they could not ascertain the identity of the new arrivals. They heard the outside door flung open and amidst raucous laughter they heard Gonzales and Luke return.

'How did you git McCoy?'

Dan was startled when he heard the voice. He turned to Howard.

'Matt Pickering,' he whispered.

'Picked him up by the waterfall,' answered Luke. 'And won't he git a surprise when he sees what you've brought in.'

Footsteps hurried to the door. Dan and Howard stepped back as the door flew open to reveal a grinning, triumphant Luke.

'We've a visitor to see you, McCoy,' he snapped.

Dan moved slowly to the door. Luke grabbed Dan's shirt, pulled him forward and propelled him into the room.

'Don't keep a lady waitin',' he yelled.

Dan staggered forward, stumbling against a table. He stared in amazement, hardly able to believe his eyes.

'Babs!' he cried. 'What–?'

His question was halted as Barbara rushed forward and flung herself into his arms.

'Dan, Dan,' she sobbed.

Dan glared over her shoulder at the three rustlers.

'If anything happens to her I'll get all three of you,' he warned through clenched teeth.

'You won't git the opportunity,' snarled Luke in Dan's face as he tried to pull Barbara away.

Before even Dan could react Gonzales leaped forward and pulled Luke away. He spun him round and crashed his fist into the cowboy's face, sending him reeling across the floor. Anger flamed in Luke's eyes as he went for his gun, but the whip in Gonzales' hand was already snaking out to jerk the gun from the holster before Luke could touch it.

'I told you not to drink so much,' he hissed. 'You'd better take this brother of yours in hand before he ruins our plans,' he advised Matt.

'Take no notice of him, Matt,' snarled Luke. 'He's refused to jump the herd until it reaches the south end of the pass.'

Matt looked surprised. He turned to Gonzales. 'Why break our original plan?'

'Because the game's up here and with this big haul on top of the other we'd be better clearing out. I'll take this herd straight to the border.'

Matt was thoughtful for a few moments. 'Guess you're right,' he said. 'The game's up all right; we can't go back to the Bar X now.'

Luke leaped forward, grabbing his brother's arm. 'Matt, Matt, what are you thinkin' about takin' orders from this Mex.' His eyes blazed in drunken fury. 'You forgit it was our idea in the first place. We saw the opportunities in Wayman's Ford and we risked our necks killin' Wayman up in Kansas and forging the bill of sale. You fergit–'

The words were cut short as Matt slashed his brother across the face. 'Shut up, you fool,' he snapped. He spun round to face Gonzales. 'Git them out of here. They've heard too much already.'

Dan could hardly believe his ears at Luke's outburst, but as the door slammed behind them he whispered half to himself: 'It all adds up.'

The sun was lowering in the sky when the three prisoners were roused by great activity outside.

'Looks as if the whole camp is moving out,' observed Dan as he gazed from the window.

'What will they do with us?' asked Barbara anxiously.

'It's hard to tell,' answered Dan putting a comforting arm around his wife's shoulders.

'But after what we heard they—'

Dan cut Barbara's words short. 'I guess we know too much fer our own good, but I've one hope – Gonzales isn't a killer at heart.'

'Good job thet Luke ain't in charge,' grinned Howard wryly. He turned to the window again, 'It shore looks as if they're all pullin' out.'

'It's the herd they're after,' muttered Dan.

'But they won't jump it now, it's nearly dark,' puzzled Barbara.

'They'll wait until morning,' answered Dan. 'Luke said they'd planned to take it at the south end of the Pass. The Broken U will have spent today gettin' through the Pass and will camp at the south end. This mob will take up position tonight and jump it at first light.'

Howard stared desperately out of the window. 'We've got to warn them,' he whispered.

Their thoughts were interrupted as the door burst open. They spun round from the window to see a reeling Luke standing in the doorway. Alarm showed on Barbara's face as she glanced at Dan. The look did not go unnoticed by Luke, who grinned.

'It's all right,' he slurred, 'I ain't got my gun, jest thought I'd look in to say I'd see you in hell.'

He turned to stagger out again and Dan, seizing the opportunity jumped forward yelling to Howard. They sent Luke spinning across the floor to crumple up against the wall.

'Come on, Babs!' Dan called, but as he turned the outside door burst open and Matt Pickering, Colt in hand, faced them.

Barbara stifled a cry and their hopes sank as they stared at the grim-faced rustler. He glanced at the still form of his brother.

'Thet fool was warned to keep out of here. Good job I saw him come in. I ought to get rid of you here an' now but I've promised Gonzales there'd be no killin' here.' He motioned with his gun. 'Now, git back in there.'

Dejectedly the three prisoners shuffled back into the room. A few moments later shouts and yells brought them to the window where they saw the Bar X outfit accompanied by the Mexicans ride past the corner of the building.

'Guess that's that,' groaned Howard as the last rider passed. 'What happens to us?' He was about to turn from the window when Dan stopped him.

'What's this?' whispered the Sheriff.

They saw Matt Pickering return, halt, and glare in the direction taken by the riders before calling the two guards. Pickering leaned forward from the saddle and spoke urgently to the two Mexicans. He nodded in the direction of the house and handed something to the guards who grinned and nodded their understanding with no uncertain delight. Pickering straightened in the saddle and kicked his horse into a gallop in the direction taken by the rest of the gang. The guards watched him for a moment and then walked slowly back towards the house chattering eagerly.

'I don't like this,' muttered Dan. 'Pickering's up to something. Hanging back to talk to these Mex wasn't fer fun.' He paced the room anxiously.

As the guards peered through the window grinning evilly, Barbara was aware for the first time that they were young, handsome men. She started as a plan for escape crossed her mind.

'Sit down, Dan,' ordered Barbara in a whisper. Dan looked at his wife in surprise. 'Here, beside Howard,' she added hastily. 'There's a chance of getting out.'

Dan looked puzzled but did as he was told. He glanced at Howard and both tensed themselves, watching for the slightest chance of escape. Barbara strolled to the window, and taking off one of her riding boots, raised her arm.

'Don't,' called Dan. 'They'll shoot as soon as you smash the window.'

'That's a chance I'll have to take,' she replied, and shattered the glass with one blow.

The Mexicans, startled by the noise, spun round, fingers on the triggers of their rifles. For one brief second Barbara expected to hear the crash of the rifles, but nothing happened and she leaned forward smiling.

'What ees the idea?' asked one of the Mexicans, puzzled when he saw Barbara calmly stoop and replace her riding boot.

'I'm tired of talking to these two,' she replied as she straightened up. 'I want to talk to two young handsome Mexicans.'

She breathed a little more freely when she saw them relax, grin at each other and proudly straighten themselves.

'The Señora ees very pretty herself,' commented the taller of the two guards. 'It ees a pity such beauty should soon be no more.'

Barbara looked alarmed at the announcement. 'What do you mean?' she asked.

The Mexican grinned and shook his head.

'I hope that awful Luke Pickering won't be back,' said Barbara trying another line of approach for information.

'No one will be back,' answered the tall Mexican. 'They all go and leave us to do the dirty work.'

'What's that?' asked Barbara casually.

'We have to burn the place to the ground, Mister Pickering says.'

'What about us?' gasped Barbara.

'You go with it,' announced the Mexican grimly.

Barbara gasped. So that was why Pickering turned back – he had bribed the guards. This was not Gonzales' plan. Her brain reeled and then she was aware that the small Mexican was speaking.

'It ees a shame that such an attractive Señora should die this way without serving some pleasant purpose first.'

Barbara jumped at the words which gave her a lead she had hoped for. A smile flashed across her lips as she leaned forward alluringly.

'Need that be so?' she whispered encouragingly.

The Mexican was so surprised at the suggestion behind the words that for a moment he did not speak.

'You are handsome enough to capture any girl,' she continued suggestively. 'I hear you Mexicans are great lovers. It is a pity I will not know before I die.'

The Mexicans looked at each other. 'There ees plenty of time before daylight,' said the tall one.

'And there's not much use in wasting it,' added Barbara quickly, her eyes flashing their meaning to the two Mexicans.

Dan leaped to his feet, amazed at the suggestions thrown out by his wife. Protestations sprang to his lips but Howard pulled him back.

'Quiet. Babs is up to something,' he whispered. 'Listen.'

The smaller Mexican was speaking. 'When I go round to get her out you keep them two hombres covered from here.'

His companion grinned and nodded.

Barbara moved casually towards the bed and picked up her neckerchief. 'Dan, get him when he opens the door; Howard, grab his rifle and get the other one,' she whispered urgently. She turned back to the window, the neckerchief in her hand.

'We can't move with thet gun coverin' us,' whispered Howard.

'Babs has somethin' in mind, jest do as she says,' replied Dan quietly.

The two lawmen tensed themselves as they heard footsteps approach the door. The key grated in the lock and still the rifle pointed at them. Barbara leaned forward on the window and as the door handle turned dropped her neckerchief. The tall Mexican automatically stooped to pick it up and as the door swung open no rifle covered the prisoners. Dan dived at the Mexican's legs, sending him crashing to the floor. Howard leaped at the same time, grabbed the rifle and spun round to face the window. The Mexican outside, startled at his companion's yell, straightened quickly, but before his finger could close on the trigger Howard fired, hitting the Mexican between the eyes. He turned to Dan's assistance but found that Dan had already dealt effectively with the Mexican.

Dan jumped to his wife's side. She flung herself into his arms and burst into tears.

'It's all over, Babs, darling,' comforted Dan. 'That was a fine job you did.'

After a moment Barbara straightened, brushed away the tears and smiled at Dan.

'Come on,' he said, 'let's check the horses.' He paused to relieve the Mexican of his colt before they all hurried to the stables where, much to their relief, they found their horses.

'Guess Gonzales left his two hombres to take 'em out,' remarked Howard.

Dan nodded. 'Howard, you take Barbara out of here when it's daylight; I've got to git to thet herd.' He picked up his saddle and threw it on to his horse's back.

Howard and Barbara protested vigorously but Dan shook his head.

'It will be no place for a woman, Babs, an' we can't leave you here on your own. Howard, I'd like to hev you along, but you'll be doin' a good job an' settin' my mind at rest if I know you're lookin' after Babs.'

'Guess you're right,' said Howard. 'You needn't worry.'

As soon as the horse was ready the sheriff armed himself from the Mexicans, said goodbye to his wife and Howard, climbed into the saddle and was soon out of sight in the gathering darkness.

Chapter 15

Dan rode swiftly to the end of the valley where his search for the narrow cleft, through which Gonzales had brought him as a prisoner, proved harder than he expected. He cursed the delay, but once he found it he lost no time in leading his horse through. Dan comforted the animal as the roar of the waterfall grew louder. He paused on the flat rock behind the fall whispering comforting words to his horse before carefully picking his way over the wet, slippery rocks. Once he had cleared the waterfall and reached more even ground, Dan mounted the black and moved steadily along the valley.

The difficulty of following the rustlers' trail in the darkness made progress slow so he quickly gave up the idea of following them. He pushed his horse forward into a quicker pace, determined to reach the pass as soon as possible and work his way along to the herd.

He reached the fork where Curley had thrown him temporarily off his trail, but after twisting from one valley to another he realised he was lost. He glanced angrily at the clouds, cursing them for hiding the stars, but he pushed his horse onward trying to use the lie of the terrain as a guide. The night wore on and Dan ached from the roughness of the ride. He began to despair of ever reaching the pass when suddenly rounding a bend he hauled his horse to a halt.

A fire flickered in the darkness. The leaping flames revealed the remains of a meal and close to the fire a cowboy, rolled in his blankets, had his back to Dan. The sheriff swung quietly to the ground, and drawing his Colt from its holster, stepped stealthily towards the sleeping figure. Reaching the man, he dropped quietly on to one knee and dug the muzzle of his Colt hard into the sleeping man's back.

'Don't move,' ordered Dan sharply.

The man stirred but froze as the sheriff pressed the gun harder into his back. Dan rose to his feet.

'Git up,' he snapped.

The man scrambled to his feet, throwing his blankets to one side and turned to face his attacker.

Dan gasped as the firelight revealed the lone cowboy. He slipped his Colt back into its holster and leaped forward with a yell.

'Clint!' He grasped the leather-faced deputy by the shoulders. 'Am I glad to see you; but what are you doing out here?'

Clint was equally surprised when he saw Dan. He slapped the young sheriff on the back.

'An' I'm mighty relieved to see you.'

Suddenly the smile vanished. 'Where's Howard?' he asked anxiously.

'He's all right,' reassured Dan.

'Good,' answered Clint. 'C'm on. I'll soon hev you some coffee.' He kicked the fire into a blaze.

'I could do with it, but hurry it up; we'll hev to ride,' said Dan.

Clint straightened from putting the can on the fire. 'What's wrong, Dan?'

'Gonzales an' Pickering are goin' to jump the herd at daybreak.'

'What!' Clint whistled with surprise.

Dan quickly related his story.

'I'm right glad to know thet Barbara is

safe,' commented Clint when Dan finished. 'Bill Collins will shore be relieved.' He proceeded to put Dan in the picture regarding the shooting of Wes Bridges. 'Took us all our time to persuade Collins to stay when he came up with us. He figured right about Pickering comin' into the hills but Pickering must hev fooled him by ridin' West before turnin' to the hills. Bill wanted to be in here lookin' fer you an' Barbara especially when it was daylight an' the herd started to move through the pass. I figured one man could do better an' I knew these hills so he agreed to stay watch on the herd.'

'Good,' said Dan, hastily finishing his coffee. 'Now you can use your knowledge to git us out of here. We haven't got long.'

The lawmen quickly stamped out the fire, packed Clint's belongings and swung into the saddle. Clint led the way swiftly and surely. The going was hard and became harder as they started to climb, but Clint pushed on unhesitatingly. Dan, glancing upwards, saw the skyline high above them. He wondered where Clint was leading him, but he did not question the older man's direction.

When Clint reached the top of the hill he pulled his horse to a halt. As Dan drew alongside him he pointed downwards.

'There it is,' he whispered. 'We're about half way along. Figured I'd use an old trail I knew an' save a few miles.'

Dan grinned and nodded, mopping his brow after the hard climb. 'Where do we git down?' he asked.

'Should be a path about a hundred yards to the south,' answered Clint and slipped from his saddle to lead the horse carefully forward. Dan followed suit and soon the lawmen were descending the narrow rocky path to the valley. Not a word was spoken as they picked their way cautiously downwards and they breathed more freely when they reached the bottom without mishap.

'Reckon we hev just about an hour,' said Dan. 'Think you can reach Jack an' the others in time?'

'Shore,' nodded Clint.

'I'll go and warn the Broken U and you be ready to ride in when Gonzales strikes. If we play this right we'll git 'em all.'

'There'll shore be a surprise waiting fer 'em,' grinned Clint and climbed into the saddle. He raised his hand and pulled his horse round to push it into a gallop, keeping close to the hillside.

Dan acknowledged the salute and without waiting to watch Clint swung into the leather and headed south.

Gonzales led the way across the hills towards the south end of the pass, keeping a pace which conserved the strength of their horses for the hard ride which would face them once they had jumped the herd. He spoke to no one and Matt Pickering, who rode alongside the Mexican, remained silent, more to satisfy his own desire than respect for the Mexican's wish for silence. Luke watched them both in anger, longing for a chance to run the show himself.

Two hours before daylight Gonzales called a halt in a small hollow. He swung to the ground and called both Bar X riders and Mexicans around him. As they swung to the ground the sound of an approaching horse brought Colts into the hands of the rustlers.

As the lone rider appeared over the brink of the hollow Gonzales laughed. 'Put your guns away,' he said. 'This is Pedro.'

The tension eased and when the Mexican jumped to the ground in front of him Gonzales spoke. 'Did we guess right, Pedro?'

'Si,' panted Pedro. 'The herd lies right at the end of the pass.'

'Good,' observed Gonzales slowly. He turned to the men who clustered round him. 'A short climb from the top of the hollow will bring us to a position over-looking the south end of the pass. The herd lies on this side of the valley close to the bottom of this hill. If we jump it correctly we can drive it southwards for the border.'

'I figure we should–' Luke's sentence was cut short by his brother.

'Shut up,' he rapped. 'Gonzales is runnin' this.' He turned back to the Mexican. 'What's your plan?'

'Luke, with five men, will go into the valley and will attack the herd driving it away from the pass. At the same time, five of my men will be in position on the hillside overlooking the camp. They will keep up a fire to keep the cowpokes quiet whilst Luke rides in. The main party, who will be here in this hollow, will ride straight over the hill to pick up the herd as it's driven forward by Luke and keep it moving fast.'

'Thet seems all right to me,' commented Matt. 'The important thing is to all work in together at the right time – remember that, Luke,' he added eyeing his brother carefully.

'Shore,' muttered Luke.

'There's one thing I'm not happy about,' pointed out Gonzales thoughtfully.

'What's thet?' asked Matt.

'We don't know if McCoy and Collins came into the hills alone. There may be others about. Pedro, anyone else down there but Broken U?'

'No,' answered the Mexican.

'Good.'

'They could be on the other side of the pass keeping tag on the herd,' pointed out Matt Pickering.

Gonzales looked thoughtful.

'If you'd let me handle it I'd hev found out from McCoy,' spat Luke contemptuously.

The Mexican ignored the remark and raised his hand to silence the retort which sprang to Matt's lips.

'Pedro,' he said quietly. 'An hour's scouting on the other side of the pass.'

Without a word the Mexican leaped into the saddle and was soon lost in the darkness.

Gonzales issued orders swiftly and five Mexicans melted quietly into the night to take up positions overlooking the herd.

'Luke, you move into position half-an-hour before dawn. Matt, come with me. The rest of you relax and await the signal of the man on the rim of this hollow,' ordered Gonzales indicating the man silhouetted against the night sky.

As the rustlers settled down Matt Pickering rode with Gonzales to overlook the Broken U outfit and to wait for first light.

Pedro slipped quietly down the hillside and kept in the shadow of the hill for a mile before riding swiftly across the valley. He knew these hills better than anyone else in Gonzales' gang and knew just the place where a bunch of cowpokes could hole up for the night. He climbed the hill steadily and rode for a further mile along the top before slipping quietly from his horse. Pedro moved stealthily forward up a slight incline, pausing every now and then to listen. Before reaching the top of the slope he dropped to the ground and crawled forward Indian fashion.

At the top of the incline the ground dropped sheer for one hundred and fifty feet and curved away on either side, dropping gently down to the level below, thus forming a natural sheltered basin. Cautiously Pedro peered over the cliff-like rim. His serious face split with pleasure when he saw that his guess had been right. Below him, out of sight of the valley and the hills on the other side of the pass, a camp fire burned brightly revealing sleeping forms. Pedro counted them silently and was about to slip away when he changed his mind. He had plenty of time before he need report back and if the cowboys moved it might pay dividends if he knew about it. The Mexican settled down to watch.

Clint Schofield waited until a slight turn in the pass afforded him some form of cover before turning his horse away from the hillside. It would not do for any of Gonzales' outfit to notice any movement across the valley, so he moved swiftly and cautiously. He urged the untiring animal up the hillside and turned in the direction of the encampment. After half-an-hour's riding the ground began to rise.

Clint was in the act of turning his horse away from the incline to circle round into the camp, which was hidden from view by the rise ahead, when he was startled by the sight of a saddled horse champing the sparse grass near some huge rocks a few yards away. Clint checked his horse and slipped quickly from the saddle. He hurried cautiously to the horse and grunted to himself as he noted that it had been ridden hard and that the saddle blanket was of Mexican design.

'One of Gonzales' outfit, I'll stake,' he

muttered to himself. 'Must hev rumbled the camp. Guess he'll hev to be stopped.'

Before choosing a suitable hiding place close to the horse, Clint unfastened the saddle but left it on the animal. The minutes seemed like hours as Clint waited.

Suddenly a figure rose from the ground about a hundred yards away and hurried towards the horse. He gathered the reins and stepped into the stirrup. The saddle slipped and Pedro crashed backwards to the ground. Before he could recover from his surprise, Clint, with Colt in hand, leaped forward and crashed the barrel of his gun across the Mexican's head. The deputy sheriff slipped the weapon back into the leather, disarmed his victim, dragged him to his feet and threw him across his horse's back. He quickly collected his own animal and was soon rousing Jack Collins and the posse from Red Springs.

Eager to clash with the rustlers, they broke camp and moved up the hill to a position of advantage across from the herd.

Chapter 16

Keeping under the hillside, Dan galloped quickly in the direction of the Broken U outfit. His eyes strained, probing the darkness in an attempt to locate Gonzales and his gang, but all was still. He rode grimly onwards casting anxious glances to the eastern sky.

Suddenly he hauled his horse to a halt. He slipped quickly from the saddle, and with his hand over its nostrils, he led the animal deeper into the shadows. His eyes narrowed, piercing the gloom in the direction of the movement which had caused him to stop. Dan gasped and cursed his luck. A few minutes sooner he would have missed the five cowboys who were leading their horses quietly into the valley. The rustlers were moving into position!

He looked round desperately, realising he must act quickly if the herd was to be saved. His horse was useless to him now that these cowpokes barred his path. His only hope was to slip past on foot. Hastily he tethered the animal in the shelter of some huge rocks and moved forward, slipping silently from boulder to boulder, moving up the hillside to round the cowboys. He passed by undetected and realising that with only five men in the valley, the rustlers must be dispersed, he moved cautiously along the hill.

The low moan of steers grew louder as he neared the herd and started to work his way down to the valley. Dan froze in his steps as he rounded some rocks into a slight hollow which ran along the hillside. Not five yards away a Mexican lay with his rifle overlooking the herd below. In a flash Dan grasped the set-up. Strategically placed in this hollow a few men could pour an intense fire into the camp whilst the five men rode in. He guessed that the rest of the gang were close at hand ready to move in once the herd was on the move.

Dan drew his Colt and stepped forward. His foot stubbed a loose stone, sending it rolling downwards. The Mexican spun round, a cry springing to his lips when he saw the sheriff. Dan leaped forward, stifled the cry with his left hand and crashed the barrel of his Colt across the Mexican's head. The lawman grabbed the rustler before he fell and lowered him gently to the ground.

Dan crouched over the man listening carefully in case their brief encounter had alarmed others.

Satisfied that all was well, Dan dropped to the ground and crept Indian fashion out of the hollow. He moved swiftly from boulder to boulder and reached the valley close to the camp. Any moment he expected a signal which would release Gonzales' outfit upon the unsuspecting camp to which he now crept. He could not afford to alarm the guards so, awaiting his opportunity, he slipped quietly past them into the camp.

Reaching the nearest cowhand, he shook him gently but urgently. Startled, the man opened his mouth to shout but the call was stopped as Dan clamped his hand on his mouth.

'Sheriff McCoy,' Dan whispered quickly. 'Don't make a sound. Where's your boss?'

The urgency in the sheriff's voice convinced the man and Dan eased his grip.

'Thet's him, close to the fire,' answered the man, nodding towards the bulky form rolled in blankets.

'Rustlers; rouse the others quickly but quietly,' Dan ordered and slipped away to alert the foreman.

The trail-boss glanced anxiously to the

east as Dan told his story.

'We won't hev long to wait,' he commented, nodding to the sky where it was already paling.

Swiftly Dan issued orders and the Broken U riders hurriedly arranged their blankets to give the appearance of still being in use before deploying themselves in advantageous positions.

Suddenly a volley of shots poured into the camp from the hillside, but following Dan's instructions the trail herders did not reply but awaited the expected riders.

Light was filling the valley when the five cowboys headed by Luke Pickering, with guns blazing, galloped towards the camp. Dan waited until the last moment before giving the signal. The first volley of shots brought three riders crashing to the ground. Luke half checked his horse with surprise but gave it its head and yelled to the others to keep going. They flattened themselves along their horses' backs and were through the camp before the Broken U could re-aim.

Dan yelled orders, and as four cowboys returned the fire of the Mexicans on the hillside he jumped to his feet and raced for a horse. He leaped into the saddle, and whirling the horse round, stabbed it into a gallop after Luke and his sidekicks. The rest of the Broken U were hard on his heels but the three rustlers had already hit the herd. Frightened by the shooting, the steers readily turned as the Bar X rustlers yelled and blazed with their Colts.

Dan urged his mount faster when he saw Pickering drop two Broken U men who were guarding the cattle. He glanced anxiously round. Where was Gonzales? What had happened to Clint? Already the herd was beginning to race before the rustlers. Dan gasped as he glanced up the hill. Riders poured down the hillside, urged on by two figures on the hilltop whom he recognised as Gonzales and Matt Pickering. In a flash he grasped their plan to ride on to the moving herd and hold it in a controllable run.

'Over there!' yelled a man who raced alongside Dan.

Relief crossed the sheriff's face when he saw Clint, heading the posse from Red Springs, galloping from the other side of the valley. The two rival groups raced off the hills and across the flat country for control of the herd.

Dust swirled high from the pounding hoofs of the steers and Dan kept losing sight of

Luke and the Bar X men as they rode backwards and forwards across the herd urging it onwards. Bullets spanged through the dust cloud as men appeared and vanished. Suddenly a figure materialised out of the dust close to the sheriff. Luke and Dan recognised each other in the same instant. Pickering raised his Colt but Dan was on top of the rustler before he could squeeze the trigger. He hurled himself from his horse, his arms encircling Pickering as his shoulder thudded into Luke's chest, crashing them both to the ground. Dan released his grip as they rolled over and sprang to his feet. As Luke staggered up Dan drove his fist into Luke's face. The rustler reeled and Dan leaped after him, but Luke twisted and turned to send Dan crashing to the ground. Luke yelled triumphantly, jumping on to the sheriff as he sprawled in the dust.

Luke's grip tightened on the lawman's throat. Dan was aware of the hatred in the fiery eyes and the triumphant glare across the thin evil face. Dan's brain pounded as the breath was choked from his body. He struggled to get an arm free from Luke's legs which straddled him. His head began to swim. Suddenly he realised his hand was free. As he jerked it sideways his hand touched the warm metal of a Colt. His fingers closed around its butt. He felt the life being driven out of him when there was a great roar in his ears. He never remembered pulling the trigger, but as he felt the grip on his throat relax he was aware of a surprised look on Luke's face which slowly relaxed into a dull glassy stare. Dan pushed and Luke rolled sideways to lay still in the dust which rose in a swirl around them.

The din of bellowing, stampeding cattle boomed in Dan's head. He struggled to his feet and was aware that the cattle had turned and were pounding towards the hillside. A riderless horse galloped alongside the steers. Dan sprang forward, grasped the trailing reins and pulled the horse to a halt. He sprang into the saddle and turned to search for Clint.

Clint had held the posse in check until he saw the way the rustlers were working. As soon as the herd was on the move and Gonzales' men appeared over the hill, Clint called to Brooks.

'I'll take half and head the herd off and turn it back towards the hill and the rustlers. You take the rest and hit the herd side on.'

Clint kicked his horse into a gallop. The posse split and earth flew as hoofs pounded the ground. The deputy flattened himself on the horse knowing he must head the herd before Gonzales ran it into full flight. Some of the rustlers were already falling in behind the steers. Clint glanced backwards and saw Brooks' party were close to the herd. He must play his part within the next few moments or all would be lost. The rest of the men sensed the urgency and spurred their horses faster.

Clint judged the line of approach nicely. They were about a quarter of a mile ahead of the leading steers and were starting to cross their path. He yelled to his horse and the animal lengthened its stride, its hoofs flashing across the ground. When he reached the desired position, Clint pulled the horse to a dust-raising stop and whirled it round to face the cattle. Men milled around him and spread out. They eyed Clint sceptically as the steers hurtled towards them. He seemed to be waiting too long but suddenly he let go a blood-curdling yell, firing his Colt at the same time.

Guns blazed as they held their line in front of the pounding cattle. Several steers dropped, others screamed in pain as the bullets flew. They faltered, frightened by what lay ahead, and yet men urged them from behind. Steer pushed upon steer. Men yelled; bullets whined. As the cattle tried to get out of the way of the men who barred their path, Brooks struck them at the side. They turned to the only way left and ran towards the hill.

Clint called to several of his men and put his horse into a gallop round the herd whilst the others, aided by Brooks' party, attempted to control the stampede.

The rustlers were still trying to turn the herd in their favour when Clint and his riders hit them. Confusion reigned. Gonzales tried desperately to rally his men, riding to and fro yelling encouragement, but the onslaught by the men from Red Springs was too much. The rustlers turned and fled.

The tall, lithe Mexican was still trying to turn the tide when Jack Collins rode alongside him and struck hard with his Colt. Gonzales slumped in the saddle and Jack quickly brought the horse under control.

'Let them go!'

Clint was startled by the yell in his ear. He turned angrily but his face brightened when he saw the sheriff.

'Dan!' he shouted, hauling in his reins.

'You all right?'

The sheriff nodded as they pulled to a stop. 'Got Luke. Seen anythin' of Matt or Gonzales?'

Clint shook his head. 'Been too busy,' he grinned.

'Brooks appears to hev the herd under control,' observed Dan standing in his stirrups. 'And those Mex will be useless without Gonzales,' he added when he saw Jack bringing in the Mexican.

'Seen anything of pa?' asked Jack anxiously as he rode up.

'Nope.' The lawmen shook their heads.

Jack looked around, a worried frown creasing his forehead. Suddenly he started.

'There he is!' he yelled, pointing to a group of boulders half-way up the hillside.

Bill Collins appeared from behind the rocks. He was astride his horse dragging someone behind him at the end of a rope. The cowboys shoved their horses forward to meet him.

'There's Matt Pickering for you,' he grinned as they pulled up in front of him. 'I saw him attempt to escape and I figured he should pay fer kidnappin' Barbara.'

'And fer murderin' poor John Wayman,' added Dan.

The dust-covered cowboys stared at him incredulously.

'We always thought there was something queer about the way the Pickerings came by the Bar X. Reckon we'd never hev known if Luke hadn't let it slip,' he explained. 'C'm on, let's take these hombres to town and see if Howard's looking after Babs,' he said as he finished his story.

They put their horses into a steady lope and caught up with Barbara and her brother at Wayman's Ford. As they splashed through the water Bill Collins called to Dan.

'Reckon there'll be no more trouble here. I'll buy the Bar X and Wayman's Ford can be used free of toll.'

The publishers hope that this book has given you enjoyable reading. Large Print Books are especially designed to be as easy to see and hold as possible. If you wish a complete list of our books please ask at your local library or write directly to:

Dales Large Print Books
Magna House, Long Preston,
Skipton, North Yorkshire.
BD23 4ND

This Large Print Book, for people
who cannot read normal print,
is published under the auspices of

THE ULVERSCROFT FOUNDATION

... we hope you have enjoyed this book.
Please think for a moment about those
who have worse eyesight than you ...
and are unable to even read or enjoy
Large Print without great difficulty.

You can help them by sending a
donation, large or small, to:

**The Ulverscroft Foundation,
1, The Green, Bradgate Road,
Anstey, Leicestershire, LE7 7FU,
England.**
or request a copy of our brochure for
more details.

The Foundation will use all donations
to assist those people who are visually
impaired and need special attention
with medical research, diagnosis
and treatment.

Thank you very much for your help.